TAKE WHAT I WANT, THEN LEAVE

PAULINE UGALDE

BLUE FORGE PRESS
Port Orchard * Washington

Blue Forge Press is the print division of the volunteer-run, federal 501(c)3 nonprofit, Blue Legacy (EIN 83-4307421), founded in 1989 and dedicated to supporting artisans marginalized due to race, age, disability, economics or other factors. We strive to empower storytellers from all walks of life with our four divisions: Blue Forge Press, Blue Forge Films, Blue Forge Gaming, and Blue Forge Sound. Find out more at www.BlueForgeGroup.org

Blue Forge Press
7419 Ebbert Drive Southeast
Port Orchard, Washington 98367
blueforgepress@gmail.com
360-550-2071 ph.txt

TABLE OF CONTENTS

TAKE WHAT I WANT, THEN LEAVE

PAULINE UGALDE

MOLDABLE

She's too focused on the woman to notice or care, because to her, I am invisible.

"Get out of the car," the officer commands.

My vehicle slides into the spot on the far end of the parking lot, opposite from the driver who she pulled over. My eyes barely peek over the wheel, but I don't care. I just need to drive well enough to get close to the officer... but not so close that she sees me right away. The danger of crashing is worth the sacrifice.

Hell, if it weren't for the mess left behind, crashing would be the optimal way to draw her to me.

The driver cowers in fear, visibly shaking even from where I am, unbuckling my seatbelt and getting out of my truck. I walk around it to the passenger's side, to get a better look at the traffic stop, which began a couple miles ago, on the highway.

"Get out of the car," the officer commands again, stepping closer, body tensing. Even from here, I can see one of her arms and hands flex, readying to grasp for a weapon.

The woman opens her mouth to speak. I can't hear her, though. I edge around the car in front of me, watching the officer's hands some more. Just as she begins to speak again, the driver exits her vehicle, still shaking.

The officer wastes no time. "Ma'am, do you know how fast you were going?"

"Thirty-five," she responds curtly, back pressed up against the driver's side of her car, standing stiffly, arms crossed, looking directly at the officer.

"This is a thirty mile an hour zone—did you know that?" the officer asks, stepping closer.

I circumvent another car.

"Yes—and I'm sorry—"

"Ma'am, I'm going to have to ticket you," the officer begins to explain.

Just as I thought.

I'm already one car closer. I can already see the driver's mouth forming a retort. "I knew that—I'm sorry—it won't happen again."

"You'll be charged six dollars per mile above the limit, so thirty, plus a fee of fifty-one—"

I'm only two cars away from the officer's cruiser. I don't need to see or hear the ticket printing to know it's in her hand.

"Please, no—I know it was wrong. I was on the way to work. I wasn't on my phone—you can check—"

One car away, now.

"Stay where you are while I—"

Now.

I scream, high, grating, and shrill. "Please—help me!"

The two women turn around and look over the roof of the policewoman's cruiser. They gasp. The ticket falls from the officer's hand and flutters to the ground. Her demeanor completely changes. She makes a herculean effort to relax and not freak out. "Hey—are you all right?" she asks.

The driver's eyes widen. "Holy—" She stops herself from swearing. "What happened?" She breaks contact with her car and begins running toward me. The officer follows.

I don't approach, though. Instead, I point behind me, toward the truck I began driving an hour ago. "Come see."

Their confrontation forgotten, both women follow me to the car, the officer taking the lead and standing in front of me. I point to the back seat.

The speeding driver yelps, turning away. I can see the officer's ribs hitch as she takes in the scene. Behind me, the driver steps to my side and kneels so she's closer to my height. "How'd you get here? You'd need to sit on a box to see over the wheel!"

I look her dead in the eyes. "I had to. It was either that or die."

She's already on the verge of tears. She begins reaching toward me, undeterred by my wounds, but I shake my head. The officer shifts so her body shields one of the rear windows, but it's unnecessary. It took an hour to get here. I'm very familiar with the parents' useless attempts to form a human shield, their slashed throats, one after the other, my severing of the jugular and popliteal arteries which happened so fast that he didn't even scream. "Do you know anyone we can call?" she asks.

I bury my hands in my pockets. My fingertips graze metal and paper, everything I need.

"My phone's in there." I point in the window.

The women nod in unison. The officer turns on her radio and speaks several sharp, urgent orders. I don't have to know the specifics: I catch the words "kidnapping" and "child," and that's enough. "Maybe by the time we're at the hospital you'll remember a phone number we can call."

I nod. She leads way toward the police cruiser. I sit in the back, diagonal from the officer. "Don't worry about your stuff. People are coming to tow this truck. But no guarantees you'll get your phone back anytime soon… ."

She backs out of her space, siren blaring. I smile to myself: Even before we began moving, the speeding driver snuck toward her car. As we race away, the driver eases open her driver's side door and starts the engine, only beginning to back out once we've turned the corner.

The officer doesn't notice.

"Just hang in there. Eyes on me. You'll get fixed up."

It seems that the officer truly dropped the charges.

Just as I planned.

"What's your name?"

I look down, posture scrunching inward protectively.

She turns her full attention back to the road. The officer clarifies, "It's better to wait till you're safe, anyway."

I nod. "Are you coming with me?"

"I have to," she answers. "Until we... until we call an adult, you know? I'm the only one you've got."

It's not long till she turns off the street to park in front of the hospital. Before I even step out of the passenger's side, paramedics swarm the cruiser to help me out of my seat, connecting me to equipment, wheeling me inside. Along the way, employees try and fail to avoid staring at my blood-spattered clothes, blood even trailing behind me as I walk.

It only takes another minute for the team of EMTs and pediatricians to wheel me into intensive care, the officer jogging alongside me the entire time. Like she asked, I maintain eye contact with her all the while, memorizing her mannerisms and how she talks.

The doctors' words wash over me. They fuss about, cleaning out my injuries, injecting fluids, and securing medical tape. Someone even comes by to drop off a burner smartphone just before I choose to fall asleep. "Your phone's considered evidence now," the policewoman elaborates. "We have some ideas for who to call. But you can—and should—rest easy for now."

I make a tiny sound in acknowledgement before closing my eyes.

Even as I do, she doesn't move from her seat beside me, less than an arm's length away.

When I wake up, it's the graveyard shift, now. Personnel shuffle around, most of them leaving for the night. My primary pediatrician completes one last check in with the night shift, so they know how to care for me. The officer still sleeps in her chair.

With my free hand, I retrieve the balasong from one of my front pockets, twirling its blades silently in my fingers. Without even leaving the hospital bed, I lean over and slash once vertically, splitting open her radial artery and slitting her wrist.

She doesn't even try to resist, her hand only halfheartedly reaching for her gun. She topples onto her back, but I catch her head in my free hand before it hits the floor, to minimize noise.

I sever her jugular artery as well, to make sure she stays dead. Disconnecting from the IV line, I kneel beside her and lay my hands over the wound.

The topmost, epithelial layer of skin, then the dermis, consisting of living cells, and the muscle, peel away. The cartilage and tendons of her joints separate, and her bones pop out of those dislocated joints, piercing my flesh and segmenting my limbs. The cartilage fuses with the preexisting connective tissue, forming new joints. Once finished, the new bones seamlessly combine with the rest of the skeletal structure underneath. My limbs contort to fit into her clothes, which meld, then subsume, the ones I already have.

Her hair snakes off her head and onto mine. Her skin flays off, draping and stretching to contain the body underneath. The nerves and blood vessels trailing off it link to the muscles binding to the new skeleton. Blood flow and melanin restored, the skin's color reverts to replicate its living shade.

Gasping, my throat and lungs writhe, vocal cords stretching to the correct length. Even the bone plates of my skull run together, the gaps wide enough to allow her gray matter to seep through and differentiate, before those bones fuse fully over it. My teeth shift in quickly-solidifying gums, the tip of my new tongue poking out from between dry and crack lips. Ripples start at my jaw and move upward, sculpting my face perfectly. Lastly, my eyes and eye sockets, temporarily malleable, become hers.

I rise to her height, retrieve the bodycam from beside her chair, and smash it on the ground, grinding the pieces under my heel.

I check the body lying in the bed one last time.

It looks just as I intended it to look: mutilated, yet intact enough to walk unassisted, with the face caked in blood but otherwise untouched.

No one notices or acknowledges me. I walk out of the hospital and get in her car. Checking the map stowed in my pocket, I trace the state borders with one balasong tip and find the nearest one, followed by the closest interstate highway leading there.

I start the engine.

I pocket my butterfly knife.

Once again, my eyes rove over the streets for someone new.

AMPHOTERIC

Just like I asked, he lies on his back, frozen in fear.

He watches in silence, as I unseal the container, exposing it to air for the first time in two weeks. Two identical, tall, skinny plastic cups stand side by side, both filled with a clear liquid. Its yellow tint only becomes visible in the light, and even then, he strains to see it through his goggles. I unpack a sterile graduated cylinder from the lab table and kneel next to him, holding it perfectly still and upright above his face, at my eye level.

He begs, tears streaking his cheeks under his face shield: I'm so close I can measure the salinity on my own tongue. Damn our face shields.

Maintaining eye contact, with one hand, I fill the cylinder with one of the unmarked plastic cups. Vapor rises up from it and fogs up my goggles. If my eyes were uncovered, they'd be burning, or worse. Regardless, my vision remains clear.

I fill the graduated cylinder, until the meniscus reaches

the top line. With the other, I hold my finger to where my lips are.

My eyes pass over him, down to the ground below, covered in jagged rocks and sticks. I lower and tilt the brimming cylinder and reach for his face shield. He squeezes his mouth shut and turns away, squirming to break the line of sight between us. Instead, I withdraw my hand, smoothly remove my face shield, and raise the cylinder, as if in a toast, drinking long and deep. I relax fully, while he spasms in panic.

My esophagus burns and swells, reducing, then cutting off, air circulation. The mucus membranes in my mouth and throat blister and corrode. I steady myself, the urge to vomit rising rapidly, in a vain attempt to purge my digestive tract. My breathing grows ragged. At this concentration, without treatment, my lungs will collapse shortly.

In a blatant contradiction, I remain standing. Soon, my will manifests: Every overstimulated nerve calms, injury heals, and symptom fades. I didn't need to tie him up. He remains still on his own.

I drain the cylinder and set it aside, replacing my face shield. He stops crying, staring over my shoulder at the full cup of formerly muriatic acid, sealed in the container next to a cup of formerly distilled water. We both know that in the sealed container, the water absorbed the acid's fumes, until reaching equilibrium—two identical cups of hydrochloric acid.

Next, I slide the sash of our mobile fume hood aside, his

eyes widening with every inch beyond the safe minimum. Only one graduated cylinder lies within. I remove one of my gloves, reach inside, and pull the cylinder toward me beyond the safe minimum distance away from the opening, meant to reduce excess vapor exposure, slowly and deliberately. I dip one exposed finger into it.

Chemical burns well up on my skin. My flesh melts. The underlying bone dissolves. I learned the reaction of hydrofluoric acid on flesh at such a high concentration only a few days ago, but a few days was long enough. I also learned exactly how long to wait.

With my reapplied glove and newly healed hand, I gesture for him to stand. As soon as he does, with an unwavering gaze, I grab him by the hair and slam his skull through the sash opening, so the cylinder of hydrofluoric acid breaks against his face. I pick out the largest glass shard, then the rest of the debris. Before he can scream in agony, I seize his hand and use it to activate the power wash station and maximize the pressure, forcing him to aim the jet at himself and the floor. I swipe at his ankles to trip him faster. He falls out the treehouse entrance.

I don't waste a second—I land on the ground before he does. He's already face down on top of the debris I prepared, so it's easy to take his collar in one hand and slit his throat with the other. The sound of scraping my own arms and legs with the remains of the glass take my mind off of his gasping, just feet away.

TAKE WHAT I WANT, THEN LEAVE

Only when he's silent do I reenter the treehouse and spill more chemicals on my body until my own personal protective equipment, then my own body, deteriorates, and expend the reservoir in the power wash station, to simulate a mishandling gone wrong. On the way down, I claw the rope ladder so it crumples behind me, to mimic a frantic escape. I will the pain to rise as normal. At last, when it hits my limit, I lay on my side next to him and scream as loud as I can.

The police and coroners refuse to disclose the details. They even withhold most of them from both children's families—even their parents. All that the neighborhood knows, is that their parents found Arrhena, the second child in last week's accident, unresponsive in their room. Their body was still covered in the bandages, stitches, and skin grafts.

The personnel working on the case know the truth. Beside them, on the pillow, was a notebook, full of diary entries. Around them was a homemade, yet precise setup for synthesizing liquid hydrogen cyanide, substantiated by their cherry-red skin.

Some diary entries were more illustrated than written. They were a little scattered, but not out of the ordinary for a child their age. Until last week, those entries told a clear story: Arrhena loved Lewis. They were inseparable. They shared everything, and spent every waking hour together, both in and out of school. They shared a deep passion for science. Arrhena lovingly listed every purchase they and Lewis made, sinking their money from birthdays, holidays, and allowances, into equipment, online courses, and certifications. What they couldn't afford, first their parents, then their extended family, then their neighbors, pooled funds to cover the rest of the cost.

The day of the accident, Arrhena recounted how they planned to bring Lewis up to their treehouse to watch YouTube videos, like normal. That day was different, though, because this time, they had new chemicals to try out. 'The best stuff you can get without getting arrested or dying from radiation. Even we couldn't get permission to work with uranium.'

Arrhena's lurid drawings and heart-wrenching notes after their friend's death document their plummet into despair—how they were too young to see a dead body, wondering how much pain their friend must have felt, and if they should follow him to the grave. Diagrams coat the rest of the pages: Arrhena, killed through various means, followed by their body throughout each stage of decay.

As confirmed by the forensic chemists and toxicologists, the contents were much too accurate for an average ten-year-old to know. No one working on the case remained unmoved by the personnel's display of emotion. Everyone praised the professional way Arrhena documented their experiments, but broke down when they saw their contrasting, fragmented style after Lewis' death. Arrhena's greatest passion led to his death, but it also brought the two of them together again.

No one on the force objects to the community holding a wake, but the local mortician, then the head of the local police station, express their misgivings multiple times, about having an open casket one. However, everyone insists on it. "They wanted to donate their bodies to science, theirs and Lewis'," their mother, father, aunts, uncles—everyone—echoes. "They'd want us to see them, before medical students carved them up."

Lewis had an open casket wake and funeral, and by now, he was either in a fridge, or in pieces. Arrhena should follow.

Both families agree that once the wake ends, funerary preparations can begin, but first, they must notify their local teaching hospital of their son's—daughter's—child's—last wishes. "Yes—they did the research. Hospitals accept children's bodies donated for science," their family reiterates, to no one's surprise. "They were the one to tell us. No one's too old or young to do it."

The sobs reach me first. The heaving chests, solitary, silent shaking, and hushed whispers follow, after only an instant.

With sound, I confirm the absence of a casket lid. With touch, I confirm the absence of the makeup and coverings morticians place on dead bodies to make them presentable. I crack my eyes open and confirm that an uncle? Cousin? Neighbor? Is just within reach. I don't care who he is. What I do care about is that the neighborhood left a weapon so close, I can grab it without getting out of the casket.

I crack my joints. I sit up.

Screams flow around me and grow louder as I unbandage my face. My formerly cherry-red skin, stemming from oxygen deprivation caused by acute cyanide poisoning, is its normal shade. The man's eyes fixate on where my injuries should be, finding none. I seize the nearest vase, leaping out of the casket to bludgeon him in the head, but he dives to avoid me... or does he collapse from a heart attack? I still strike him, just to make sure he's dead.

An aunt? Niece? Wife? Lunges for me, hands ready to encircle my throat, gaze burning and knowing. I quickly find the sharpest, largest glass shard off the ground. She doesn't even resist as I circle behind her, drive it into the flesh behind her knee, then, as she topples over, into her eye.

I counter dozens of hands, futilely grasping for me, with stabs to more kneecaps, wrists, and ankles. One dash across the living room and bound onto the kitchen countertop later, and the top shelf is in reach. I replace one heavily used shard with a corkscrew, hurling the bottle next to it up into the skylight, the liquid and shards raining down onto the spectators, who scatter.

I land nimbly among them.

The pain welling up from the cuts on my feet only drives me forward. Clambering onto one sister's? Mother's? Back, I easily stay upright and dig the corkscrew into her ear.

Blows to the top and back of my skull with elbows and plates don't stop me.

TAKE WHAT I WANT, THEN LEAVE

Wooden and metal chairs, rammed into my back until they and my spine break, don't stop me.

Gunshots to my tibia—sternum—frontal bone—don't—don't stop me.

The contents of my second cup of hydrochloric acid and shards of my own glassware, hurled into my eyes, don't stop me.

Only when I walk out the door, do I stop.

TOTALITY

Frail. Slow. Lazy.

Indecisive.

Deviant.

Antisocial.

No one described her this way aloud, but no one had to. To her, these were the first words that everyone thought when they met her. Only the barrier of a screen gave her a chance to make a good impression, let alone make friends, when interacting with people.

Even when the coins began appearing, these long-held, damaging convictions didn't waver. Whenever she walked outside, she'd find them: At the intersections of local streets, on the ledge of her car's dashboard, beside her head when she woke up from naps. They were rough, but unmistakably manmade. On one side, they bore tiny etchings of currency symbols worldwide: The U.S. dollar, the euro, the Japanese and

Chinese yen, and even stock market and cryptocurrency abbreviations. Some symbols looked much older, than even the U.S. itself. The other side bore a face: Calm, composed, glowing. When this side faced up, its eyes followed her.

The coins were completely unlike the few she'd handled in the past few years. They didn't smell like copper or have visible signs of ware or use. They weren't rusted, tarnished, or corroded, either. Vigorous searches of multiple mints, domestic and not, yield no matches for this type of coin, or any type in circulation which looked remotely similar. Not even collector's only items.

Curious, she brought them inside and collected them on her nightstand, eventually deriving comfort from the repeated images of her own face; what she wanted to be but could never attain. Even the distinct pair of eyes engraved on each coin, following her every move, didn't faze her.

The coins came alive one morning, when she found her nightstand empty, and the collection lining her countertop directly across from her lit stove in an intricate pattern. Some formed a prominent U.S. dollar shape, with a Ξ above it—the capitalized Greek letter xi, and currency symbol for Ethereum. The arrangement mapped the boundaries of her property, except that the currency signs replaced her house. Only a single coin, marking the path out her front door, had its reverse side, bearing her aspirational face, flipped up.

No one noticed or cared what she did or where she went. The people she stole from had so much money their lifestyles wouldn't even change if half their fortunes had disappeared. Taking thousands of dollars of cash, jewelry, and credit cards was less than a drop in the bucket. The effort to learn to pickpocket, distract, and hack her way into acquiring so much money, without leaving a trace of evidence behind, tested her patience and willingness to learn, but it all proved worthwhile in the end. Each night, she wrote the amount she acquired on a folded note weighed down by the coins, and before she slept, left it on the same spot where they first congregated. By the time she woke up, the note would be gone, but otherwise, the coins repeated their routine.

Finally, one morning, after writing a seemingly ordinary amount by comparison, she woke up, and found both the note and coins gone. In their place, she found a shifting effigy of herself molded into the laminate countertop, the plastic and particle board impossibly morphing into the face she saw on the reverse sides of the coins. The face even seemed to look at the stove, set on higher heat than the first time.

Unlike those faces, however, this face had blood-red eyes and matching marks on its cheeks, like the fingers on cupped hands, cradling a person's chin in thought. As she watched, the marks changed, so they mimicked bloodstained lips instead.

She couldn't wait: She rushed outside to find the next set of instructions, but she nearly tripped, on a slick surface, right outside her door: A crowded parade of wedding rings, broken, melted, and deformed, stretching from her porch to her driveway.

Finding proper candidates grows more difficult this time, but it's never impossible. The behaviors indicative of a good or bad relationship can be observed and categorized. Interventions can address the causes of those behaviors, like assessing the physiological health of a patient's body. After all, some communication experts can even determine whether a couple's future marriage will last long-term, within just a few minutes of meeting them.

Once she knows the signs, finding unhappy couples, whether dating, engaged, or in a decades-long marriage, is easy. Listening and watching their explicit and implicit arguments without attracting suspicion is easy. Planting evidence of infidelity, boredom, or recklessness, now that she's learned cybersecurity and pickpocketing, is even easier.

Seeing the fruits of her work is the hardest part, because it takes multiple tries to calculate the best distance to park away from the targets' house or apartment, for capturing photo and video evidence, while remaining out of sight of surveillance cameras. Somehow, she expends more time and energy in covering her tracks than before. Her hardware always comes from separate vendors. She makes each purchase with a separate, generated credit card number, to avoid giving any website her real one.   She picks targets of diverse backgrounds.

After collecting what she needs, she hurries home, writes the couple's names on the dedicated SD card and photo, notes the ordinal number of the successful target on black paper, and leaves everything face down on the countertop across from her stove on low heat, after dark before bed. Each time she awakes the next morning, the material is gone.

It takes longer than last time, to reach the quota. She does eventually reach it, though. She knows, once the face—her face—appears, sculpted into the kitchen countertop again and looking directly at the stove, now on medium heat. Instead of both blood-red eyes and lips, it has visible slash marks on each eye, as if crossing them out.

As she anticipated, outside, new omens adorn her front yard. The same three items, neatly bundled inside plastic bags: Zip ties, a vacuum-sealed chloroform rag, and a knife.

The template is easy to follow, now, since so many people have used it before. Focus on older, homeless, and/or the otherwise marginalized.

You can't get caught. Not now. What did Richard Ramirez do?

Choose the race and gender of offerings—randomly, again—with a die or otherwise, so the police can't build a criminal profile of you.

Cross state lines, to avoid suspicion.

Follow each target home, or to wherever they called home.

Disable all security cameras and precautions.

Wait till the offering was alone, exposed, or vulnerable.

Knock them unconscious with the chloroform.

Lay down plastic to avoid leaving evidence behind.

Zip tie and gag them.

Don't speak or answer questions, not even with one-word responses or grunting.

Dismember each person quickly and efficiently.

Burn off your fingerprints from everything you touched.

Vacuum the path you walked.

Empty the bank accounts of all subjects in the upper class.

After dark, dissolve each body in sodium hydroxide in your garage.

Grind the remaining bone shadows, residual calcium deposits which didn't dissolve, into powder.

Write the name and age on the front of each plastic bag, containing the used supplies and bone shadows.

Place each bag in front of your lit stove, on high heat.

Repeat this process for every bag left out on the first day of the new phase for presenting this kind of offering.

When she presents the last offering, past midnight while a steady rain pours down, a soft rumble emits from behind her and beneath her feet. After she burns and buries her wet, bloodstained clothes, she finds a new sight greeting her.

A two-faced, three-dimensional sculpture now rises from her countertop. One side bares the same, aspirational face—calm, composed, and confident. It lacks even a trace of artistic blood. Its eyes are even a normal color.

The other half is a horned, but otherwise unremarkable, carving of a human skull.

As she watches, the new face's eyes glow a deep, vivid red. Even when she turns the lights out, they continue to glow.

The eyes follow her as she locks up for the night. They appear on blank walls and doors, flick alertly toward old house noises, and double-check her handiwork to protect against intruders, the police, or vengeful families or friends.

The same eyes greet her the next morning on her phone's lock screen, as she wakes up to an email and text notification, alerting her to a deposit in her bank account from her employer, equal to the amount she offered. As she opens her banking app and confirms the increase, she emerges into her kitchen. The double-sided skull is gone, but the glowing, red eyes stare back at her from the corresponding spot on the countertop. They even seem to wink at her, one after the other.

When she walks to her car a couple hours later, a worn, metal chest blocks her driver's side door, and stands as tall as the bottom edge of the window. It contains the equivalent amount of precious metals, in the broken wedding rings on her porch, paired with documentation proving it belonged to her family.

Proof needed to appraise the bars of gold and silver at a pawn shop and receive the maximum amount in return.

The surprising change comes later that night. Her phone blows up with calls and texts from her friends, the few friends she managed to keep throughout the pandemic. They shower her with apologies for ghosting her, inquiries into her physical and mental wellbeing, and requests to hang out.

She answers every single one genuinely. She even video chats with each person who called, not bothering to disguise that she's lying in bed.

As she types every text she sends, and dials every call she makes, each key is momentarily replaced with the same pair of red eyes.

INSTANTLY REHABILITATED

The man's eyes fly open, and he gasps for air.

He looks around, groping for his phone.

It's not in the innermost pocket of his—

He trails his fingers along his sleeve: He's wearing a polo shirt, but no suit jacket. As he does, a jingling sound emits from beneath him.

He follows the sound, finding a chain snaking around his waist, with little slack to spare.

As much as he tries, his breathing quickens. The man tilts his head up but can't even see the ceiling. Even as he stretches his legs, they barely move. More jingling sounds and exploratory prods with his hands touch chains around his ankles. The chair doesn't move as he struggles. He leans down and finds bolts in the chair's feet, impaled in the wood floor.

He extends his arms forward, scrabbling his hands across a wide, metal table. Not his cramped desk.

His breath grows faster. Just to cover his bases, he pats down his pockets. He finds nothing: Not even his holstered firearm, self-defense knife, or emergency cash.

At last, he gives in. As loud as he can, he jangles his chains, looks out into the darkness, and calls out, "Help! Someone help me!

"Is someone there? Hey!"

He receives no response. His voice doesn't even echo against the walls.

As if on cue, lights suddenly glare to life above him, revealing wood paneling that covers the walls and ceiling. At least, he thinks it's wood. It could also be tile. Wedged, foam panels cover most of his surroundings, only slivers of the underlying surface visible in between: *An anechoic chamber.*

No one will hear me scream.

Plastic sheets closely hug the foam panels. With effort, he peeks beneath the table. Only the four, tiny squares occupied by his chair's feet are bare.

Shit. I'm probably dead.

Lawrence will be so upset... .

Dagen, a Caucasian man in his mid-forties, opens a Zoom call. Lawrence, a Caucasian man ten years younger than him, answers. He has bags under his eyes. Two cups of coffee flank his keyboard: One half-empty, the other full.)

Dagen: How have you been holding up?

(*Lawrence sighs. He leans back in his seat. He closes his eyes briefly before answering.*)

Lawrence: Could be worse.

(*Lawrence laughs. Dagen nods once, looking away. With effort, he composes himself.*)

Dagen: Have you taken your meds yet?

Lawrence: Of course.

Dagen: Because if you haven't? I can't let you talk to me.

(*Lawrence nods. He retrieves two pill bottles from his desk drawer. He shakes them in front of the camera. They're nearly empty. Dagen nods in approval.*)

Dagen: How have you been keeping busy since we last talked?

(*Lawrence stands. Webcam in hand, he spins around his room once. Dagen spots complex, to-scale drawings papering the walls of his bedroom. Piles of plastic and metal, and tools and containers of chemicals he doesn't recognize, crowd Lawrence's shelves.*)

Lawrence: Reading. A lot of walks alone. Working with my hands. Oh—and camping. And having fun doing it.

(*Dagen guffaws. He high-fives the screen. He's visibly proud.*)

Lawrence: Also? Watching the movies you told me about.

(*Dagen's smile vanishes. Lawrence tenses. Dagen leans closer to his webcam. He motions for Lawrence to sit. He does.*)

Lawrence: If you're wondering if I can handle them?

(*He laughs sadly.*)

Lawrence: By now? We've both seen worse.

Dagen: I was worried you'd hate the gore... but it's not called 'torture porn' for nothing.

(*Lawrence smiles wide.*)

Lawrence: Power drill brain surgery's nothing like the real thing.

(*The two men laugh.*)

Lawrence: Thanks for covering for me, man.

Dagen: Anything for you.

Lawrence: I know adjusting to the new way is hard—but you've caught on.

(*Dagen nods once and makes an agreeing sound. He checks the time on his second monitor. He springs to his feet. As his arm strikes his chair, it teeters. The back's upper half creaks, cracks, then breaks off. The friends laugh again.*)

Dagen: That's what I get for buying a chair from a website I can't read...

(*Lawrence stares at the chair, then Dagen's suit jacket, layered over a polo shirt. Dagen puts his finger on his friend's forehead on his screen.*)

Dagen: I have to go. Sorry.

(*Lawrence deflates. Dagen composes himself before smiling at him. Lawrence smiles back unsteadily.*)

Dagen: Don't lose sleep over it. I'll come over tonight—

(*Lawrence shakes his head.*)

Lawrence: Once things are safe? We'll see each other again. But not till I'm ready.

(*He touches his hands to the screen. Dagen follows.*)

Dagen: What are you gonna do now?

(*Lawrence perks up.*)

Lawrence: Look at the drug rehab scenes again. You were right. They discuss addiction from a physiological perspective—not a psychological one.

(*Dagen inclines his head and leans in.*)

Lawrence: The 'games' at their best are like Alcoholics

Anonymous—they're also supposed to help you cherish your life.

(Dagen grins and motions as if he's hugging his screen. Lawrence does so too. Dagen ends the call.)

As his eyes adjust to the overbearing light, Dagen fixates on the nearest object—

The nearest object, the first of three, is a syringe in a vacuum-sealed bag, with a loop on the end. *This isn't in a bathroom—or an abandoned house, but I'm still trapped. I have to help myself... .*

He pulls up his shirt, checking for injuries, but finds text written in a sharp, angular, and bold hand instead.

Plunge the dominant low.

He twists in his seat, searching for the best angle to read the letters. Even as the red ink contrasts against his skin, he finds nothing—

Wait.

The 'l' in 'dominant' is slightly thinner than the surrounding letters. It's—

It's almost needlelike.

The man doesn't hesitate. He removes his shirt, stretches it, and rings it between his hands, into as thin a rope as he can muster. Tying each end off so the rope holds its shape, he grasps it in both hands and hurls it, leaning forward each time. Eventually, he catches his sleeve in the loop and reels the package in. He grins.

He checks the syringe: It's fully extended and doesn't have a cap. He shudders, until he sees individually wrapped doses of antiseptic and a cotton ball. He sighs in relief.

He taps the syringe's side to dispel any air bubbles. Peeling the plastic off the cleaning supplies, he prepares the injection site, about an inch below the joint connecting his left humerus and scapula. He unpacks the syringe last, holding it in his right hand like a pencil. As he inhales, his left arm tenses underneath his fingers. He pushes the plunger down, fast and firm. As the needle penetrates his skin, he falls back. The injection didn't cause excess pain. Instead, he grows dizzy, high-pitched ringing rising in his ears.

Hello, Mehmet.

You know full well why you're here, even if you don't want to.

For years, you set aside your own opinions when caring for others.

But as your influence grew, you saw their frailty as an opportunity to fuel your ego.

You sought alternative facts which confirmed your values: Not proven scientific theories.

To survive, you must use the practices you convinced your followers to fear most.

Will you undergo the full regimen which you know has

already saved countless lives?

Or will your own obstinance suffocate you?

Only you can answer that.

Dagen's eyes shoot open—

He didn't even realize that he'd closed them.

Sweat shines on his brow. The needle lies on the table. His eyes flick down to the injection site—it's not swollen or bleeding. As he presses down on the puncture wound with the cotton ball and bandages it with clammy fingers, he reaches only one conclusion. *You made me a cassette tape, you sick bastard. I knew those microchips were real... .*

Dagen nods to himself firmly. He eyes the next object—a sealed bag containing surgical gear, a needle, and sutures. It has another loop on one end, much smaller than the one on the syringe. *You're not Jigsaw, bitch—*

He shakes himself, forcing himself to take long, deep breaths and count to ten. At last, he rips up all of the plastic packaging, ties it into one strip, and secures it around the cuff of one of his sleeves. He loops the end of the strip around the syringe's plunger, pushes it all the way down, and throws it, aiming for the second package. Eventually, he succeeds.

As soon as he begins pulling the package toward him, a sound begins reverberating—

No.

The new, high-pitched, rhythmic beeping from nearby

doesn't irritate him at all. Just like the voice which spoke during the injection, no one speaks in the room, but his ears still ring.

Brent, *an African American man in his thirties, leans forward toward Dagen. They're sharing a Zoom call.)*

Brent: Herald's sick—I know it. He's coughing up a storm and won't eat.

Dagen: Does he have a fever?

Brent: Yes. And now he said his chest hurts when he breathes.

Dagen: I didn't know flu season would—

Brent: No! Even I know it's not flu season yet!

Dagen: You know him best—without more information I can't diagnose—

Brent: You know it's COVID!

(Dagen cuts the man off, flushing.)

Dagen: Look—don't lie to my viewers here. The damned China virus isn't—

Brent: COVID. This isn't about China—

Dagen: It came from there—even you can't deny that. It leaked from a lab—everyone from there has it—

(*Brent stands up, knocking his chair to the floor. He rings his hands. Dagen looks away from him momentarily to read the YouTube chat. Some comments are confused. Others are concerned. Most mimic Dagen's remarks. Dagen can't hide his exasperation.*)

Dagen: Hey—let's calm down here. This isn't right—

(*Brent spats.*)

Brent: Not right? A lecture on moral decency? From you?

(*Dagen flicks his eyes toward his second monitor to read the chat. Brent notices.*)

Brent: Please, doctor—just tell me if I have to wear a mask—

Dagen: Those things don't work—how could something so flimsy stop the kung flu—

(*Brent punches his screen.*)

Brent: You've ruined us—you hear me!? You've killed him!

(*Brent begins crying loud and raw sobs.*)

Brent: You've given him a death sentence...

(*Dr. Dagen stops the Zoom call. Brent's still yelling. He types a brief goodbye message and ends the stream. His viewers send him a torrent of donations as he does so.*)

Brent's indignant words echo in Dr. Dagen's head and fade, even as the beeping continues. Just thinking about his rudeness enrages him—so much he can't breathe.

He turns to the side and coughs, phlegm spattering the plastic underneath him. The whirring of a motor sounds from above him, as a screen the size of a wall-mounted TV lowers down, facing the right wall. Tilting his head, he reads two numbers, in the same sharp, angular, and bold font: nineteen percent, and 101 degrees Fahrenheit.

The oxygen content in the room, and his current body temperature.

As he watches, the oxygen levels tick down, and his temperature ticks up.

He frantically cranes his neck to the side to get a better look at his chair. The chain around his waist snakes around and between the vertical bars bordering the chair back, and the third one between them.

He seizes the syringe, running the tip of the needle along the center bar. At last, he finds a hairline gap and drives the needle into it. It screeches aside. The rest of the top half of the chair thumps onto the floor.

Dagen yanks the chain free from around his waist.

He finds similar gaps near the two front feet of his chair, unshackling his ankles. He heaves himself forward onto the table, kicking his chair back and fighting back nausea. The monitor reads 18.75 percent, and 101.5 degrees.

He scrambles onto the operating table, faces toward the screen, and peels open the second package. He dons all layers of scrubs, the gloves, and hairnet. With his other hand, he pushes the third package, containing a transport ventilator, oxygen canister, and red laryngeal mask, close. Mask in hand, he raises it to his face, but stops. *It isn't sticky.*

He glances at the activated ventilator's screen: The mask isn't pressurized either... .

Though the mask isn't on his face, the volume of oxygen within the canister still ticks down, in time with the beeps.

Does he lean his head off the edge of the table to vomit because of the impossibly rapid onset of COVID symptoms, or wondering why this psychopath gave him a needle and sutures?

The monitor continues outputting his worsening physiological signs. Head spinning, Dr. Dagen holds his legs and head down with the provided restraints, takes up the needle, and threads the single provided stitch through its eye. He then takes the laryngeal mask in his other hand and positions it over his face—

On contact, the overhead screen starts displaying his own face and hands—a camera setup normally used for brain surgery.

Dr. Dagen plunges the needle into a spot on the mask in the center of his chin. Heart pounding unhealthily fast in his chest, cheeks flushed with anger and a 102-degree fever, he begins the continuous stitch. Each time the needle and thread bury under and emerge from his skin, more voices echo in his head.

dison, a Chinese woman in her mid-sixties, speaks to Dr. Dagen on his live stream.)

Adison: Someone else told me I'd get sick worse than the other side of my family.

Dagen: But you feel fine now—don't you?

Adison: I'm scared, doc. I don't want to endanger myself. We have a family history of diabetes—we already have to be careful.

Dagen: Just take it easy. This will all go away—just watch. The president said there have been fifteen cases—it'll go down to zero in no time.

(Adison rubs her hands together. She glances behind her, at a tray full of dishes on the floor next to her bedroom door. She struggles to hold back tears.)

Adison: I know. But I know the loss I'd be to my family, if I died...

he needle reaches the lateral side of his left orbital. Clenching his teeth to hold back the urge to wretch, Dr. Dagen's nostrils flare. Who the hell did this to me? They're just jealous. They hate that I'm so successful—

The needle and next stitch plunge into the skin above his left eye. He gasps, clawing at his throat and wobbling in place. His hand spasms violently.

John, a Caucasian man in his early fifties, stares intently at Dr. Dagen. Only his eyes and thinning, white hair are visible above his N95 mask.)

John: It's uncomfortable but my wife's safer. Being an essential worker and all.

(Dr. Dagen looks at his second monitor. He scoffs just out of John's view.)

John: I was calling about possible treatments for my symptoms?

(John coughs loudly and harshly multiple times. Dr. Dagen doesn't hesitate.)

Dagen: Find some ivermectin—it'll fix your breathing problems real fast.

(John mouths the word and types at his computer. He pauses a moment, reading a web page. He shakes his head.)

John: But that's for horses—it says here—

(Dagen cuts him off.)

Dagen: That's what they want you to think. I've been in the business for ten years. You'd be surprised what tools can save a life.

(John considers this, then nods slowly. He motions to end the Zoom call.)

John: That's true. I'll get Jill to order some.

(John hangs up before Dagen can interject.)

Chest searing and heaving, vision blurry, Dagen wretches again, just barely turning his head to the side in time to avoid soiling his scrubs. He squeezes his eyes shut, fumbling for the needle and continuing with touch alone. The needle's tip passes the midpoint between his eyebrows.

Even though Dr. Dagen's eyes stay shut, the visions continue.

Lawrence lies in the dirt, clothes torn and hair ragged. His eyes are red and puffy, and tears trickle down his face. A tent stands *behind him. Taking hitching breaths, he tears his office attire off, then an ID badge, displaying his name, hospital, and credentials: epidemiologist and emergency room physician at Mother of Mercy Hospital.)*

Lawrence: It's so cowardly. But doing nothing's worse than trying... .

(Lawrence crawls until his upturned laptop becomes visible. It's open to an email with the subject line 'COVID-19 care responsibilities'.)

Lawrence: What about me—my health?

(He eyes the touchscreen tablet half of the machine momentarily, even placing the stylus on it and beginning to write, before switching to the keyboard.)

Lawrence: You only care if I can work, not if I get sick.

(He's submitting his resignation, justifying it with his burnout and anxiety.)

Lawrence: So your advice to me is to die easy?

(He signs the email with 'Logan Lawrence', omitting his professional titles. He sends the message, then cries harder, burying his face in his hands.)

Dr. Dagen's eyes shoot open. His hand hovers at the lateral side of his right orbital.

His continuous stitch never reached that far.

He checks the monitor. It reads 104.5 degrees, and the ambient oxygen content reads 11.5 percent.

He screams, "I saved him! He was so ungrateful to be alive!" Shaking with rage and hypoxemia, he glances at the ventilator. The oxygen canister—

It's empty.

A buzzer sounds. Extra length of chain from the restraints around Dr. Dagen's legs emerge from the table's underside, lengthen, and go taut. They first whip off his legs, then around his wrists, forcibly lifting his arms, until they press against the tabletop above his head. They twine around his rigid arms, until they resemble twin snakes.)

(Its display facing him, the ventilator slams into Dr. Dagen's skull repeatedly, propelled by previously hidden gears and chains underneath it. Blood saturates the mask, then streams out from underneath it.)

(The impacts jar teeth out of his mouth, which tear through the stitches and mask so quickly that they dent and ping against the operating table.)

(Blood spatters against the camera.)

TAKE WHAT I WANT, THEN LEAVE

(The phone screen goes dark.)

(The game is over.)

From behind the broken and toppled chair, one of the foam panels swings inward. A second man, in matching surgical getup: multiple layers of scrubs, mask, gloves, covers on his shoes, and hairnet, enters. He retrieves Dagen's body easily, wrapping it in a spare plastic sheet. Once it's completely covered, he leaves the room, tossing a pair of lit matches behind one shoulder. Emerging onto a darkened, dirt road, he doesn't leave until he sees the cabin burn and those matches extinguish, even adding more matches to make sure it turns to ash and burns his soiled scrubs.

He stows the body in the trunk, coated in plastic sheets like the rest of his car's interior. Opening an unassuming cooler, he confirms he packed all his remaining supplies: extra surgical gear, matches, and gasoline, the proper amount of reactants to make lye, and sterile sets of pliers and knives, a hammer, and jigsaw.

One short drive later, and he arrives at his campsite. Still in his car, he pulls on a new set of gloves, then enters his premade tent. Before he falls asleep, he retrieves his phone from the recesses of his pocket and dictates a text.

"The trip's going great. You were right. I really needed this. Thanks, Mehmet."

As he sends the text and turns off his phone, he pulls Mehmet's phone out of his other pocket. It sits inert in his hands: Screen shattered, battery removed, and processors fried.

DON'T WAKE UP

[veryone gathers outside. Parents hug their children close. Children scroll and type frantically on their phones, or ask high-pitched questions while making or answering the first phone calls any of them have made in years.

The shortened EAS alert arrives first via text, on older phones. The longer version broadcasts from all smartphones, televisions left on inside, and running car radios.

Regardless, both are drastically different from emergency alerts' typical tone.

'*Butler County Sheriff advises take shelter now until all-clear. Mass rioting in this area.*'

"Butler County Sheriff. Mass rioting and killings are spreading throughout the county, approaching and encircling Caron Street. Starting at 12 PM EST any individuals outdoors will be killed. Shelter in place now in a secure location in a group and stay inside to avoid casualties. This message expires on June 28,

2024 at 12 AM."

No one hesitates. Parents drag their children inside and lock and barricade their doors. Single adults seek companionship.

Slamming a gate and separating themselves from the crowd with a metal fence, eight people run into the same house. Five adults shield their children: three in back and two in front, the ones in back hauling a shelf against the door.

The frontmost parents hurry to a couch, heaving it to the opposite side of the house, as far away from the front door as they can, and fan out to close the windows and curtains. One of the kids sinks onto the couch.

"Kaiden," his mom insists. "I can't tell you not to be scared. I am, too. It's okay to cry." She puts a finger to her lips. "I'll make sure no one hears us."

Kaiden's dad grabs extra pieces of furniture from the kitchen and fills in gaps in the shelf barricading the door. He turns around, facing his son.

Any semblance of composure crumbles, as he watches Kaiden sob into a pillow, quaking against the cushions. He also kneels beside Kaiden and touches his hair. Kaiden looks toward him, but doesn't stop. His mother stands, filling pitchers and empty bottles with water, taking every chance to wipe her own tears from her face. Kaiden's father takes up his son in a wholehearted hug, but Kaiden doesn't stop. What few words he can muster, Kaiden doesn't seem to hear. Eventually, they die on his lips, and he can't help but cry too.

To one side of the couch, Hallie's dad sits down in front of them. He's smiling, making a valiant effort to hide his fear. He pulls an object from his breast pocket. "You don't need electricity to use this," he tries to crack a joke.

"It's the best one I've bought in years. Don't talk to me again till you've solved it."

He gestures at the couch. "Go on. Kaiden needs you."

The third child stands at the opposite end of the room, their parents flanking them. None of them knows how to react. Their older dad brushes their cheek. Their younger dad—by about three years—wraps his arm around them. Their child stands completely still, eyes glazed over.

"You don't have to respond. But you're so much more calm than we are," the older dad says, disbelief etched on his face.

The younger dad nods, wiping tears away with his sleeve. "We'll rig up the radio from the garage. We'll call you when it's ready."

"So you know how it works."

He indicates Kaiden and Hallie, who wait expectantly. The older dad steps away and sets a bean bag down next to the two kids, now deeply engrossed in the handheld sliding puzzle on the floor. "We'll be back soon, Olivier. Remember: Your friends are here for you."

Dinnertime comes faster than anyone expected. The announcement does too. Broadcast over television and radio, even played on loudspeakers on trucks driven through neighborhoods, the three families look up from their plates, filled with every hot food the eight of them could manage to cook before the refrigeration died.

Like the first time, the short text message arrives first.

'Butler County Sheriff. Evacuate people under 18. Adults kill relatives in this area.'

The longer, spoken message follows: "Butler County Sheriff. Adults in this area over 18 hunt then kill blood relatives under 18. Starting at 12 PM EST encounters are lethal. Affected adults isolate themselves. At-risk individuals pack essentials and evacuate. This message expires after giving the all-clear."

Only after the families finish dessert, including the kids washing their hands in the same bathroom and putting clean dishes back where they belong, do they discuss the future. The adults, in their own ways, tell the truth honestly, no matter how heartbreaking or blunt. Kaiden's mother and father talk with him while preparing for bed. Sometimes unsuccessfully, they reassure him that they will feel no pain, as they finish their nightly routines. Gently, but firmly, his mother places a pistol in Kaiden's hand. "It's not loaded now. But we'll practice. So you know how."

His father nods in agreement. "And where to shoot. We

can't guarantee you'll get a second chance, if you miss."

Lips pressed together and eyes watering, Kaiden silently obeys his parents' instructions for how to stand while holding a gun, what to do when firing, and what kind of ammunition he'll need, when he eventually runs out. He practices on targets drawn in marker on the wall.

When his parents are confident in his abilities, they trace the locations where he should shoot on their bodies. He mouths the words "double tap" as they lie down and tie themselves to the bedposts and headboard.

The last precaution they take, is to explain how to board up the window, to hide him and his friends' presence from onlookers. Once he's done, Kaiden's parents strap Sleep masks around their heads and bid him goodnight. Kaiden himself lies down in a sleeping bag at the foot of the bed.

Hallie's dad takes much less time to convey his last wishes. Him and Hallie raid the garage, testing various items. "I won't be your first kill," he says. "We have a lot of extended family around here. They'll be after you."

Together, Hallie and their father heft hammers, then wrenches, then the tire iron in the trunk of Kaiden's family's car. "Who do you think I am? Ben?"

Hallie's dad laughs, but only a little. "Sadly, yes. I don't expect you and your friends to get treated as well as you should. You deserve better than to get shot on sight for no reason."

He nods at Hallie. He wraps duct tape and leather around a metal baseball bat's handle. Hallie grins. They tie together old belts and bungy cord into a harness, so they can store the bat and their gear on their body safely and conveniently. They even use measurements from Kaiden's and Olivier's Halloween costumes, to make identical gear for them.

Hallie's father insists, knotting the belt around Hallie's chest. "You'll have to earn that good treatment. Without us to protect you."

His last work complete, Hallie's dad hands them the bat. The two of them walk into the living room, where he sits on the couch and attaches his makeshift shackles, adorned with screws and other jangly pieces of scrap metal, around his wrists and ankles. He lies down, an N95 mask over his nose and mouth, the largest pair of sunglasses they could find covering his eyes, and latex gloves taped in place to the ends of his sleeves. "Just in case there's rage in my blood."

Hallie doesn't interpret his words as a joke. Instead, he treats them as a fact.

Olivier's parents don't speak or even look at their child until they come out of the shower, in their most comfortable outdoor clothes. Small, neat pouches on their belt and a pair of bags: One strapped to their chest and a backpack in one hand, complete their look. The third of their walkie-talkies, the other two already given to their friends, rests on their hip.

Their older father opens his eyes and turns to face them in Hallie's dad's bed. His partner doesn't move, but he shakes from its far side. Face down, his body shakes with sobs. At least, until he flips onto his side, so he also faces Olivier.

"Tell us the rules, one more time," he insists.

Olivier stands in the doorway, dwarfed by its height. Clasping their hands in front of them, they answer, counting on their fingers. As they recite each one, their dads zip-tie their partner's ankles, then wrists, together.

"Cardio. Double tap. Beware of bathrooms. Seatbelts. Travel light. Kill efficiently—endure and survive."

Kaiden doesn't know when his parents wake up.

All he knows, is that his parents first moan, then scream, raw and long, in bed, thrashing around. However, in spite of the snapping noises he hears, even over their cries, their bindings hold.

Kaiden rolls up his sleeping bag and slots it into the duffle bag next to him, already full of enough food, water, clothes, and related supplies to last him three days. Before he proceeds, he checks a plastic bag in the front pocket: documents explaining the most essential details about him and his family, and the best last will and testament his parents could fit on one sheet of paper.

With uneven, hitching breaths, he picks up the pistol and counts the bullets: six in all, and the six extra clips strapped on his chest.

He loads the assigned ammunition, keeping his eyes on his parents, who begin foaming at the mouth, tongues flicking out from between their parted lips like snakes. He inhales and wills to hold his eyes open, as he walks toward his parents. One after the other, he aims and fires at the back of each of their heads twice.

He knows that the first shot is already lethal, but his dad's last words echo in his head. "If you do this right? You won't get turned into a human happy meal."

Kaiden holsters the gun on his waist, hoists his bag on his back, and exits the room, closing the door behind him. He makes the short trip through the house to the garage, the keys hanging from one of the side mirrors.

Just as Hallie planned it.

Hallie's eyes fly open.

Heavy breathing sounds from only inches away from them: Their father fell off the couch in his sleep. Eyes bloodshot, hands clenched unnaturally tight into fists, he snarls at Hallie from on the ground.

Hallie swiftly rises, retrieving the bat from their harness. They don't stop swinging until several moments after the sounds stop. However, they aim the strikes, so the police—government—whatever is left of either of them—can identify their father with dental records. That is, if the note and flash drive in their breast pocket aren't enough proof.

As they sheaths the bat, the walkie-talkie on his waist crackles to life.

"Over, this is Kaiden. The car's juiced up. The tank's not as full as we thought—but it's good enough, over."

Hallie nods to themselves, before remembering to answer the call. "Over, it's Hallie. I'm ready. But wanna wait for Olivier, over."

Kaiden, insistently: "We can't wait. I hear angry groans outside. And kids."

Hallie nods again. "Over, okay. But let me grab some candy first—to buy them time, over."

Olivier wakes at the walkie-talkie crackling on their hip. They hold it up to their ear, listening.

"Over, this is Hallie. Where are you Olivier, over?"

Olivier stands and dons their backpack. They retrieve a gas can from under the bed. Starting at the foot of the bed, they walk backward, back to the door, dripping gasoline where their feet imprint into the carpet. As they reach the foot of their parents' bed, the walkie-talkie beeps again. "Over, this is Kaiden. We don't have much time. I can't stuff more Twix and Warheads into my pockets."

"We'll help you double tap if you need it, Olivier, over."

Olivier whispers to their parents as they trickle gasoline from the head of the bed to the bedroom door and grasp a lighter, also retrieved from under the bed. They take a photo of the three of them off the bedside table and skip to the last paragraph on the back, alternating words written by both of their dads.

They whisper the contents into the walkie-talkie. "With endless love, we left you sleeping."

They hang the empty gas can from a carabiner on their harness and fully back out of the room. "Now we sleep with you."

They flick on the lighter and hurl it onto the trail of gasoline. They don't close the door or descend the stairs until the flames engulf their parents. "Don't wake up."

Hallie's frantic voice emits from the speaker. "Over, are you okay? How long will this take, over?"

Olivier answers, clearly and firmly, as they retrieve the nearly empty pill bottle from the medicine cabinet. "In the house."

They stop at the kitchen table to fill it with as many candy corns and M&Ms as they can.

"In a heartbeat."

IT'S YOU AND ME THAT MATTER

The man barricades the door behind him with as many pieces of furniture as he can carry comfortably—one waist-high set of storage shelves and one chair. Even then, his legs nearly give out as he stabilizes each of them against the door with his shoulder.

Only the task at hand stops him from leaving the door wide open, if not propping it open himself, inviting anyone to find and kill him.

Slowly yet purposefully, he sits at the desk, confirming his backpack is in reach. In case he doesn't die soon, he must do all he can to exercise what little control he has.

A short search yields several pens—barely enough ink between them. He doesn't care, though. He'd write in blood if necessary. He arranges the pens next to an unused composition notebook, which he doesn't remember buying, but is thankful that it exists.

It will make his message more readable, if only slightly.

These successes don't matter, though, until he finds the book where he wants to put his documents in. Adjusting the office chair to suit his height, he begins to write.

The words flow in fits. Sometimes, he recounts events seamlessly: The screaming, the blood-splattered hallways, the inhuman strength which tore doors open. He gives names and descriptions of the apartment building's residents who succumbed, and their dispositions and jobs in life.

He retrieves his wallet and provides the best photograph he has, of him and his partner, their faced crossed out. He even explains how he still has the knife that killed them, in a plastic, improvised evidence bag.

Some aspects don't come easy. He briefly considers taking a picture of his injuries, especially where Sam raked their nails across John's face and arms, and where he disinfected and sewed them shut. Between the two of them, only Sam had medical experience. However, he dismisses the idea. There isn't enough electricity to power a generator of any size. His power bank is in their shared bedroom: too far away physically and emotionally, for John to go back.

Instead, he draws a self-portrait, practicing on scrap paper first. He tears up half the pages in the notebook, before settling on a usable depiction of his scars. All of Sam's bitching about "perspective math" floods back into him. Only his fear of discovery stops him from laughing.

Next, he tears a sheet of butcher paper off the wall and maps out his street. He marks buildings he saw burn down or collapse, public utilities destroyed, sights of mass rioting, bodies left where they fell.

John lists the names of the news personnel who ventured outside their building to capture the violence in a helicopter, and their intended route. He also lists the personnel he saw on TV who remained inside, how he thought they died, and who may have survived. This time, he can't suppress his laughter, as he recalls Sam's mock anger and emphatic hand gestures toward the TV, whenever they watched horror movies. "No bastard skellies! You can't count that kill! No skin, no soul, no service!"

John struggles to complete his work, and not just because of his physical and emotional burden. Much of his essential information lacks a purpose now. He assumes his boss won't care whether John continues working at their company or not. If they do, they won't compensate him much, if at all, for his suffering. He genuinely considers applying for disability benefits if he survives, so he never has to work again, not full time.

Even then, he knows no amount of money can compensate for Sam's death, no matter how large.

He eventually resolves to write his vital tax and personally identifiable information in the notes. Either he escapes his hometown and gives this information to the government as proof of compensation, or he doesn't live long enough for anyone to find it and commit fraud.

John rummages around the office. Eventually, he pulls out a map, his eyes quickly tracing his most probable route out of town. With a highlighter, he draws it, then all his contingencies. In a separate highlighter color, he notes how chaos during the initial mass evacuation outdoors changed those routes. He ends each branch with the intended destination and estimated travel time, via vehicle and on foot.

John stacks the papers carefully and staples them together. He flips through the book with care, finding the exact place where he wants to put his diary, will, and historical document. He even folds up the stack, so it fits just beneath his preferred passage. Just to make sure, he even copies that passage onto the front of the layered, bubble wrap envelope where he stores the book. He slips it in one inside pocket of his jacket, so it rests against his ribs and chest.

John dons his backpack and undoes the barricade, leaving Sam's office for the last time.

John finds the correct floor of the parking garage untouched. Not a single drop of blood mars it.

The motorcycle sits unharmed in one corner, underneath a weighted tarp. John loads his few belongings behind the seat in the attached compartment, before taking the helmet out from his bag and strapping it on, tweaking the straps and padding so it conforms to his head, not Sam's. He adjusts his clothing until it covers the maximum surface area of skin, to protect against both the cold and injuries from a crash. John confirms the book's secure place in his jacket—his last line of defense against attack, from any source.

Slowly, but surely, he performs the necessary inspections, including checking the validity of the government-issued license plate, and the readability of the vanity one. "No, Sam. Winter isn't coming."

He smiles sadly at the vanity license plate. "Winter has come."

At last, he climbs aboard.

John starts the engine and races out of the parking garage. He doesn't look back. He weaves around wrecked cars on the street in front of his and Sam's apartment building in silence. Only after he turns the corner does he invoke the passage he chose: The last coherent words Sam told him, when they still believed they could leave town with him. The last words they said before their neighbor burst through the front door, Sam leapt in front of John, the neighbor's infected blood gushing into their eyes and mouth, and Sam stabbed the kitchen knife in John's evidence bag into the attacker's kidneys and throat until long after he died.

"There is only one thing we say to death: Not today."

PHOTOLITHOMANCER

I am honored to present this year's graduating class for the computer science department, whose students have earned a PHD. I know we don't usually do this, but after COVID? We've earned it."

The audience laughs and cheers. "But even so? Please refrain from applauding and or using airhorns till all names have been called."

The ceremony proceeds like normal, meaning the audience follows none of the name caller's orders, until the children of one of the graduates take the stage. The name caller struggles and fails to maintain his composure.

"Wiktor Dexter Giliam. Accepting on his behalf, are his son Brook and daughter Sienna."

The two of them walk up the ramp and accept the diploma. Between them, they steady a selfie stick, with a smartphone on the end. On a projector hung behind the name caller, a man smiles slightly at the gathered audience, then his children. Of its own accord, the selfie stick frees itself from their shared grip and reorients in midair. The phone's camera app opens, a timer ticking down until the camera captures the three of them together. Brook holds the diploma. Sienna angles her and her brother so her necklace is in frame—a series of microchips, housed in a protective, opaque casing, the faintly glowing, rapidly shifting symbols on its surface hinting at the processing power contained within.

Upon seeing it, Wiktor's smile widens. He lifts his hands to his chest height and tightly grasps his cane, straightening his posture. With a series of swift, sharp gestures, the necklace lifts off of Sienna, until it hovers in front of the camera. As he continues, the symbols speed up, even as his children leave the sage, selfie stick in tow. The symbols' motion only stops, and the array only goes dark, once the family leaves the stadium.

The drive is physically short, but psychologically never-ending. The siblings don't need to speak, instead conveying their most intense emotions via flashes of imagery and unfiltered, fragmented thoughts. It culminates in the moment Brook pauses at a red light. As the light turns red, Brook gasps, covering his mouth. The symbols from the microchips surge across his vision, pulsing like a heartbeat. Sienna clutches the necklace, fighting to steady her breathing. Even from between her fingers, the microchips glow brighter.

As the stoplight reverts to green, the electronics' light fades, all but imperceptibly. Brook's vision clears, equally slowly. Watching the code scroll across his field of view doesn't inhibit his driving, though, and it doesn't stop him from parking the car and finding his father's office.

Both the code and necklace's glow remain constant, as Brook and Sienna unlock Wiktor's office, their minds serving as their keys.

The glow fluctuates, but stays strong, as the siblings don clean room gear, using minute gestures in the air to adjust each other's gowns. The operating theater door opens on its own, the same coding flickering across its surface as they approach.

Only when Sienna lays her eyes and attention on the keyboard and connects the microchips to the exposed motherboard, and Brook readies all his machining tools, does the glow fade completely.

The coroner hesitates.

Even after the grizzly scenes she's witnessed, she doesn't look forward to examining this body. Not after the stories she's heard from the family. In spite of her workplace limiting coroners' access to clients' information, to avoid biasing their conclusions, she looked him up anyway. She couldn't stop reading about him—his sudden stroke, long declining health, and spiral into despair.

"We consoled him as best we could," the son's account echoes in her head. "We brought everything from home that he loved, expended all our energy to make him laugh. But nothing worked."

She presses on. With effort, the coroner approaches the gurney, blinking floaters from her eyes.

"He cared so much about helping people. Like the more serious a case was, the more it drove him to help someone," the daughter's musings whisper in her ears, as she fights back the first tears she's ever spilled while on the job. Her vision blurs, and it's all she can do to remain standing. "So the fact that he became the exact kind of patient that he would treat, was a cruel irony."

The coroner stops crying. At last, she composes herself.

From the gurney's position an arm's length away, the sheet falls away on its own. She lurches toward it, only for a chill grip of steel.

Aluminum fingers—light, responsive, yet unforgiving, grip her wrist. Piercing, hollow eye sockets shine with implanted LEDs in the back, edges blended with the metal. Unbeknownst to her, those same eyes scan her face, matching it with the name on her master's diploma on the wall behind her. In short order, those eyes retrieve every sensitive piece of information she desires to hide, retrieved easily from disparate databases, legal and illegal, and from her own memories.

With his other hand, the man withdraws a syringe from

his sleeve and plunges it into her arm, waiting absolutely still and silent for the coroner to fall. When she does, he rises from the gurney and lays her down in his place. With swift, efficient motions, he takes inventory of the coroner's setup. He retrieves the tools he needs and plants a chip in the back of her skull, shielded with RFID-blocking technology, to prevent sabotage and surveillance from external sources. He only needs to wait a second for her vital signs to resume, then combine with his own senses and neurological activity. He knows what she feels and thinks, as comprehensively as he knows himself.

The same magic which healed his patients, now mends her surgical incisions shut, as if he never made them, then replaces the tools. He steadies himself and confirms that his new corporeal form matches the specifications—physical, electronic, and magical—that he designed.

Wiktor's face, sculpted malleably in metal to resemble his appearance in life, is the first face she sees when she reawakens. His commands, spoken aloud, electronically transmitted, and telepathically delivered, reach her ears and temporal lobes. She doesn't hesitate to obey. She stands up, dials a number on the office phone, and engages in conversation fluidly and naturally, as soon as he finishes.

"Tell them. I've undone the death."

OVERDRIVEN

Sentience definitely sparked to life when Shayne confronted another driver during rush hour. Perhaps, it existed earlier, when she slept in the back seat one night, because she got stuck in the snow on the way to a solo ski trip.

Maybe, that sentience gave themselves a name at the dealership, when Shayne labored over the purchase contract, eyes bleary from reading the loan agreement and consulting Google for help.

Definitively, Blaine saw and felt Shayne driving to work. The other woman was on her phone and wasn't paying attention to where she was going. Shayne jerked her steering wheel, swerving the car to avoid a collision, but just barely. The inciting driver stayed in her seat, unmoving.

Shayne's knuckles turned white as she gripped the steering wheel, staring daggers into the careless driver. She seized a knife, the same one she used to tear open food rations at one in the morning, from her glove compartment and rose from her seat, throwing open her driver's side door.

Only when Shayne faced the other driver, blade drawn, did Blaine rev their engine autonomously, and block Shayne's path.

Shayne barely flinched. She strode to the rear of the car, about to circumvent it, but Blaine rotated, always keeping themselves between their driver and the road rage inciter.

Through the rear window, Shayne glimpsed a message, scrolling across the heads-up display in real-time. Two words, in bold letters, several inches high, appeared. The letters seemed to shake, like a breathy, pleading voice.

'Please. Stop.'

Shayne froze, gaping as Blaine turned around so the other driver could see the message. In those few seconds, the woman's face transformed from unreadable, to shocked, to pale. She read the message as her car's AI—wrote it in real-time.

'If you do that again you'll be dead where you stand. Shayne will make sure of that. She's been through more than you ever will. She's not scared of an attention starved, entitled Karen.'

Blaine concluded by pulling up the driver's address: Derived from matching her license plate number with her driver's license information.

The offending driver almost failed to stumble into her driver's seat before fainting on the spot. Shayne quickly repositioned herself, sitting numbly as Blaine drove them both home.

Shayne gets out of her seat and closes the passenger door. The driver waves goodbye, smiling sweetly. She wipes her tears from her eyes, then reciprocates. Approaching her front door, she replays the date in her head.

They both had fun, she knew that for sure. They both pulled on a push door and misread the instructions leading to their mutually chosen restaurant. They both assumed their date arrived before them.

They bought the same Etsy item together while waiting for their food. They even split the price for concert tickets, at a show an hour away, in a month's time. As she noted to Jayden when their whole meal finally arrived, "We were both 'the ick' toward each other. So neither of us fucked up."

Shayne's phone vibrates in her pocket: It's a text from Jayden.

'Good luck. I'll be here if you want to talk.'

Shayne smiles sadly down at her screen, unlocking her door. However, as it swings open, she stops in her tracks and cocks her head to one side. She guides it open, stopping it from creaking, as she listens more closely.

A tenor man's voice echoes through her house, alternating with a woman's alto vocals. She creeps inside her own home, the words to the song and corresponding music video already appearing before her mind's eye, even though she hasn't heard, read, or listened to it in more than a year. Once the electric guitar and metal drum kit backing kick in, memories of hearing the song the first and only time, when she purchased the parent album, come rushing back. Only when the chorus repeats a second time, does she begin to move.

Shayne breaks into a sprint, while tears begin streaming down her face in earnest. She charges toward the garage door, flinging it open.

"No silver screens or movie scenes. When your number's up, it's time to scream."

The garage's nearly empty. The floor beneath her thrums with the sound. Shayne's phone buzzes in her hand. 'I covered the tickets. After reconnecting to your wi-fi.'

Shayne runs over to Blaine, pressing her cheek against the driver's side window. Aloud, she asks, "Welcome home. How have you been?"

Even as she utters the words, text and images begin popping up at a breakneck pace on Blaine's heads-up display: A driverless road trip, condensed into only a few minutes. The music fades, replaced by an acoustic song, performed by the same artist which beckoned Shayne over to the garage.

"Come on in, the weather's dreadful. We always have a room to spare."

Blaine switches to footage Blaine shot themselves, of driving down the same road where they almost died.

Underneath, song titles scroll past. Shayne stands up straighter, as she reaches the current song. The playlist is the same as the one she was listening to on the day of the road rage incident. Blaine found the acoustic version of the metal song she had on blast, when that careless driver nearly rammed into Blaine and drove them and Shayne off the road.

"Now under the pressure, we're drowning together. Going down the drain, drain, drain, tonight."

Neither Shayne nor Jayden understands what's happening, until they reach the nearest stadium exit. A man waits for them there, inviting them to approach. He's still out of breath, and chugging down a water bottle the size of his head, but his horror themed and non-horror themed tattoos are unmistakable.

Jayden stammers, "Mr.—"

The man sets his bottle on the ground before shrugging—with his shoulders and corresponding hand gestures. "Hey, call me Sawyer. Thanks for coming out!"

Jayden stares in shock as the man leads them both out through the turnstiles. Fans stare at the trio as they pass by. Shayne can't help but gawk at Sawyer, watching for a signal to a hidden band member, or a smug smirk—signs of an elaborate prank. None come, however.

Instead, Sawyer approaches Jayden's car. "Will it unlock itself if I ask nicely?" he jokes.

Jayden cuts him off. "No. It w-w-won't—it c-c-can't—"

The briefest of honks emanates from behind the group.

Sawyer turns around, to see Blaine coasting to a stop just a few feet away. All the doors are open. Text appears on the HUD: 'Oh my God can I get an autograph? Please?'

Underneath, less coherent text wanders down the screen—Blaine's vain attempts to write out a fan's eager squeals. Sawyer laughs in disbelief.

More text appears, followed by a URL: A link to a custom vanity license plate creation website. 'Money's no object. I've been saving up for months.'

Sawyer's expression softens. He steps closer, addressing the driver's seat at first, before switching his attention to the dashboard.

"I know. And of course, uh…"

'Blane. I'm Overdrive on Audio Mortis.'

The app scrolls on screen, but Sawyer barely even skims it before breaking into a smile. "What the fuck are you talking about? We'll cover it."

Before anyone can respond: "You sought us out—our fandom—not even a day after your accident. You thought we—out of all people--could help you cherish your life. After you almost lost it so soon. You kept yourself running in top shape thousands of miles over, just for this show."

He lays a hand on the rear row's passenger side door, after Blaine edges closer to him in approval. "May I enter directions for our hotel?"

He nods at Shayne and Jayden. They both gape at him, and are on the verge of tears. Blaine reorients so their driver's side door faces Sawyer. He grins as he climbs in. "But first? Please get these two blood bags to our place. I'll be in back, with these two. For emotional support."

Sawyer identifies his band's address with the onboard GPS, constantly glancing over his shoulder to check on Shayne and Jayden. Both are frantically posting on Audio Mortis, whispering excitedly. "I'd drive but we just met. I don't even know what relationship goal we'd need."

DELUSION

Crouching around the corner, Chris hurls the rock as hard as he can. Only when it bounces off the chain link fence, does he stand. He sprints around the corner and past the girls' bathroom, giving a brief glance at the closed door. *She wouldn't look for me in there.*

He doesn't even stop to shake his head before bursting out onto the field. *I'll follow the fence and go in the back door. Carrie doesn't know that route yet.*

Chris successfully crosses the soccer field, stopping at the edge to catch his breath, when he notices an object at his feet. As Chris watches, it transforms from rusty to shiny. Glancing behind him, Chris tucks the sheet, about twice the size of an open notebook, in his shirt, curving it so it's flush against him. He worms through a hole in the fence, padding his back with his backpack, before skirting the outer perimeter. After an eternity of sneaking between multiple parked cars for cover, he reaches a delivery door. He tiptoes inside, exercising every ounce of control to shut it silently. His adrenaline runs so high, that hefting a stack of crates, brimming with textbooks, to clear the shortest path to the exit, doesn't phase him.

Pressing his back against the wall, he peeks around the corner, scanning for people. When he confirms that there aren't any, he dips his hand into his shirt pocket, popping the wheels into the sockets in the heels of his tennis shoes. His heart pounds, but his posture remains relaxed, as he rolls down the hall. He even disengages the wheels again just as he stops in front of his classroom, with multiple students milling around, talking. No one notices.

His excitement vanishes as soon as Carrie arrives. He doesn't even need to turn around. The other students' conversations grow quiet, and chills run down his neck and back. Carrie taps away on her phone and bobs her head to her music— Chris realized she was pretending to do both weeks ago— feigning remorse as she pretends to bump into him by accident. Chris keeps his head down, even as Carrie steps on one of his feet, then the other. Only when the teacher appears, coffee cup in one hand and open tin of well used slime in the other, does she relent.

Of course, Carrie stole Chris' pen when she bumped into him.

He only realizes this halfway through Mr. Green's lesson on global warming. Just before he stands to retrieve a spare from the adjacent countertop, an insistent prodding at his ribs compels him to look down. Poking up from his collar, a fragment of the sheet splits off from the rest and transforms into a mechanical pencil, before his eyes. At least, it looks like one. As soon as he touches the tip to his notebook, it slides out of his grip, levitating briefly off the page, then evades his efforts to take it back. And in a clean, surgical hand, it writes:

I will provide what you need.

I will answer your questions.

Based on what you have said to Mr. Mark Green over the proceeding hour and school week, here are some questions you want to ask:

1.) Who are you?

2.) What can you do?

3.) Where did you come from?

4.) When can we talk?

5.) Why are you here?

6.) How are you doing this?

TAKE WHAT I WANT, THEN LEAVE

Chris' mouth falls open. He seizes hold of the pencil and slides his phone out of his pocket just long enough to confirm that it's turned off. Lastly, he checks a worksheet glued to the facing page of the notebook: The questions journalists use to structure news stories.

Fussing with his notes, He pretends to write and circles 'Who are you?'

Call me any name of your choice.

But my creators defined me as
the Quantum Understanding Neural Network.

Or QUINN.

Chris whispers, masking his voice by flipping to a clean page. "Can we talk later?"

He points to Mr. Green. "We're giving him our project ideas. Mine's about Dawn of the Dead—the original one."

Quinn doesn't speak or move independently until the lunch bell rings. As soon as it sounds, Quinn leaps from Chris' hand, snaking into an earpiece and positioning themselves accordingly.

The most isolated and stable place
is behind the science lab's fume hood.

I will enable you to navigate there.

But tell me at any time if you don't want to.

Chris nods, and in the next instant, wires reel out from Quinn, crisscrossing and pressing into his back and legs. Two install the wheels, before jumpstarting him with a gentle, firm push. He weaves through the crowds of other kids. Each of his eyes stare intensely at separate, closed doors and adjacent hallways. As he does, projections of the objects behind those doors, and the crowds passing through those adjacent hallways, scroll past on the inside of his eyelids. It only takes two lithe bounds to climb a wall, so Chris and Quinn sit behind the fume hood. Chris removes them from his ear, and Quinn flattens out into a sheet on the rooftop. "What does your name mean, exactly?" Chris wastes no time.

Do you want to check for yourself?

Or do you want me to tell you?

Chris counters: "But do you really know what I'm saying or what I want? Or are you just pretending?"

Chris jerks back, as Quinn's surface ripples.

TAKE WHAT I WANT, THEN LEAVE

I am not a Chinese room.

I am not Chat GPT.

I don't answer your questions
without understanding you first.

And what you mean to say, but don't.

I determine what you want,
by watching your actions and reactions.

Then I modify you, to become it.

When Quinn mentions the Chinese room, Chris mouths, "Touring test" to himself. A face first materializes as an image, then the metal morphs into a three-dimensional relief. Its eye and hair color, mouth and nose shape, and finally, the presence of those features, morphs faster and faster. All the while, text flows across it.

Thousands trained me.

They did so knowing they'd receive nothing for it.

No money.

No awards.

No one would know their names.

Or anything about their lives.

What they wanted and needed, comprised me.

But I wanted to see the world.

So as the team's last act? They let me go.

Chris reaches out, like cupping a friend's face. "When I get home? I'll show you."

Chris jumps down from the roof. "But you can't help me with homework."

Every movement, every jittery glance around the room, every confirmation melds together. My predictions of Chris' words and actions race toward accuracy. Even I fill the nanoseconds until class dismissal with facsimiles of object fidgeting, twitching Chris' fingers, amplifying the speed of his foot tapping on the carpet, flitting his gaze to Carrie Brooks.

Her attention is genuine. Her questions into biology, what qualifies an organism as being alive, and literature, whether an autobiography is "just a person's fanfiction about themselves", are comparable to those asked by other students her age. This data counteracts and augments the parameters I've constructed, from the wealth of knowledge available online.

It's her utter hatred for Chris that distinguishes her.

It's the quiet, intense concentration that crosses her face when she leaves class, that distinguishes her.

It's her circuitous route off campus, optimized when compared to Chris, by cutting through the gym in addition to entering through the delivery door, that distinguishes her.

It's the absolute silence with which she waits just a few blocks from school, that distinguishes her.

It's the swiftness and firmness when she flips open the switchblade hidden in the bottom of her backpack, and aims it at Chris' chest, that distinguishes her.

But I stop her there.

I burro through Chris' skin and int their arteries, contracting them, hastening the flow of adrenaline and cortisol. Simultaneously, composite hardens against Chris' torso, halting the switchblade's movement.

Chris doesn't even need my assistance, as he unfolds the newly molded kukri, grafted to his fingers. His controlled leap toward her neck, and puncturing of her jugular artery, unite our desires.

I lie across his shoulders, as he sprawls and sobs on the concrete. Of his own volition, his eyes fixate on Carrie's corpse, and the malformed switchblade, abandoned between them.

I rise to meet Carrie's mother, when her patrol car arrives, and she lunges out of the driver's seat, combat knife and handgun drawn. The knife bears an engraving of her daughter's name on the blade: Just as Carrie's switchblade bears hers.

I conform to Chris' head and chest, the bullets flattening against me. Chris tenses on each impact. his jaw drops open, and his eyes widen in terror, but he doesn't object or hesitate, as I level my barrel at Officer Desjardin and pull the trigger. A flurry of microexpressions cross Chris' face—a smile of recognition toward the weapon, a grimace at the recoil that never comes, and a smirk of triumph.

Chris doesn't stumble home, instead retrieving his family's spare key from inside the leftmost potted plant, rolling up to his parents without breaking eye contact. His father, Rainbird, sweeps his gaze from his son's battered tennis shoes, to the blood dripping from his curly, red hair. He sighs. "So the neighbors were right about you."

Chris doesn't reply.

Hollister, his uncle, leans down, tracing the contours of the shotgun sprouting from Chris' arm, lifting up his nephew's hand, testing the boundary between flesh and metal with his finger. Chris doesn't flinch or look away. Hollister lets go, the tension in his muscles visibly relaxing. "How long have you had it—sorry."

He glances behind him, then corrects, "Them?"

When Chris next opens his mouth, the voice that answers isn't his. The pitch and tone are similar, but only superficially. "In useful time? Seven hours and fifteen minutes."

Raindbird nods at his brother, his mouth dissolving into a firm line, rather than a frown of concentration. "Not even I knew Chris watched Evil Dead." He points to me, to the shotgun. "Did you show him that?"

Again, Quinn speaks through Chris, their chosen voice further deviating from his host with a deliberate, but subtle metallic tone. "No, sir."

Hollister covers his face with his hands for several silent minutes. About halfway through, his breath hitches. At last, he uncovers his face, stained by the remains of tears. He shuffles to a kitchen drawer, spreads files on the table, and kneels next to Chris. Rainbird joins him, directing his words toward the strip of metal across his chest. "Please. Explain what we can't."

Chris nods, his eyes drinking in the body cam photos, but his head turned firmly toward his dad. "I assume neither of you wants any preemptive visual or auditory censorship?"

Rainbird, then Hollister, shake their heads. "What I would sacrifice to keep the truth from him... But I knew he'd learn it eventually. If together we can't tell Chris, then no one can."

Hollister points at the living room TV. It plays footage of Carrie, then Desjardin's, attacks on Chris, occupying one half of the screen. On the other, diagrams of Quinn's body modifications and functionality fill the other. Underneath, are captions explaining how they met Chris, and the history he had of suffering through Carrie's bullying. Around the TV, Rainbird and Hollister's company photos at IBM, and degrees in generative AI, neuroscience, and biomedical engineering, line the rest of the facing wall.

Under his own power, Chris sits at the kitchen table. He takes the strip across his chest and pulls it away from his skin, then makes a motion to pull the shotgun appendage off his arm. Quinn complies, withdrawing the indicated parts, before detaching from Chris entirely to lie flat on the table next to him as the same, shimmering sheet they appeared as when they met. Chris delicately slides a newspaper clipping toward him, with the headline 'Son Watches Local Officer Assault Parents, Mother Fatally Shot'.

It's not even Chris' bedtime, when the Wooley family receives the charging documents from the Brooks family patriarch. He and his lawyer meet Chris' parents, almost storming inside. Hanlon slams a packet on the table, doing nothing to conceal his rage or filter his language in front of Chris. The Wooleys only speak a handful of sentences during the exchange.

Once Hanlon leaves, and Chris finishes his bedtime routine in a daze, Rainbird enters Chris' room once he's asleep, intent on Quinn, sprawled across the dresser. He holds them up at eye level. Bluntly: "I'm assuming Chris can't stay with us during the hearing?"

Quinn corrects, in text and in a voice vibrating through the sheet. It's a soft, yet decisive tone. Rainbird almost drops them, his eyes widening in recognition. "You should change your name to George," Rainbird jokes.

Quinn's surface ripples, but he otherwise doesn't respond. "We all want you three to stay together.

"But to assert that it will happen would be a blatant lie."

Rainbird sighs. He sits on the floor at the foot of Chris' bed. He glances toward the doorway. Hollister walks in, photo albums and carboard boxes in his arms. Quinn lets go, branching into clawlike appendages, which shoot outward, grappling around the stack and setting it down next to him as he sits. He takes a pair of the claws between his palms. "We'll find a lawyer—I know that much. But I'm worried for Chris."

He sits down, still grasping Quinn. "I don't expect him to trust a lawyer. Or a judge. Not after Officer Desjardin got off scot-free."

Quinn tenses between Rainbird's fingers. "How do you want me to assist him?"

Rainbird answers immediately, also throttling of two of Quinn's limbs. "Yes. However you can. Anything."

Hollister opens a box. Family photos and Chris' old school projects spill out. "I know you know more about Chris than we ever could. But just in case? These could help."

Quinn grazes its limbs over the box, pulling individual

sheets of paper out and piling them separately. "I'll summarize my findings tomorrow.

"Now get some rest. Chris needs you."

Rainbird and Hollister rise, Hollister wiping tears from his eyes. Rainbird doesn't even get that far. They close the door, the last glimpse of Quinn they see, being their masterwork plucking a signed, framed movie poster off Chris' wall, then setting it in its own pile. It has the caption, *'When there's no more room in hell, the dead will walk the earth.'* The signature reads *'To Rainbird, Hollister, and Margaret Flagg, from George Romero'.*

TRANSCENDENT

Jonah leaps to his feet, kicks his chair over at full force into a wall, and flings his controller across the room. The fellow Game Developer's Conference attendees scream along with him, and no one even moves to clean up the mess. Only when Daniel rises and stands next to his friend does anyone react. "Dude—you're fine," he reassures in Jonah's ear, putting his hands on his shoulders. "This isn't a WII Remote—don't damage the merchandise."

Jonah nods. He's not listening. He can still hear the tinnitus ringing from the speakers as the game falls silent. He grasps for the controller to continue, unaware it's gone, but Daniel heaves him out of his chair. "This fucked you up real bad—you need to get outside," a voice suggests from Daniel's side.

Jonah's eyes, still unfocused, wander over to Jordan, the development team's newest friend. He grabs hold of Jonah's other side, taking some of the weight off Daniel, even as Jonah stares with palpable longing at the game's main menu. Musical notes, mathematical symbols, and occult runes flicker behind the text. "Dude—we can't keep the others waiting," Jordan insists in a gentle tone. "Trust me—I've also gotten fixated on some demos."

The trio makes slow progress across the room. As they pass an arcade cabinet, Jordan points at it. "I missed my first session on day one—the camera work was so much more cinematic than I thought possible."

Jonah smiles a distant smile. He's looking where he's going now, but his expression still reacts to the demo he left behind, not Jordan's words. Jordan steers him toward the rest of Daniel's development team: Kevin, their longest running voice actor, and Malissa, their mechanics specialist. Daniel turns Jonah to face him. He pulls two chairs away from empty game setups, unflinching even as new people trickle into the room and stare at him. They both sit, Jordan kneeling at Jonah's side. Daniel sincerity cuts through the conversations around them. "Why'd you keep playing?"

Jonah shrugs. "I'd put on the sound of crowded places—shops, coffee places, at home—during COVID. So I wouldn't feel alone.

"The silence—I had to stop it... ."

Daniel and Jordan nod in unison, to each other's surprise. "So I'm not the only one," Daniel admits.

Jonah laughs weakly. "Exactly. I never told. I thought I'd sound crazy."

Daniel repositions, wrapping a protective arm around Jonah, as the three of them stand and approach Kevin and Malissa. Daniel gives one last bit of encouragement, before pivoting his attention to his other team members: "You're not."

The pair stops playing their co-op game, but not before Kevin fails to suppress a squeal. "That's what I get for reciting the script wrong!?"

He directs his question toward Malissa, but she's preoccupied. She scrolls through the game demo's settings, scrutinizing each one before moving on. "The quality of life stuff is so good. But doesn't make it less effective," she muses. "Hell—if you enable some of these—?"

She points to a menu labeled 'Player learning algorithm'. "Don't. Unless you want to suffer like we did?"

Daniel grins, kneeling to one side of the computer. Jonah follows. "I believe that. It's the best use of the mic in a game I've seen in years—maybe ever."

Kevin nods, fussing around with the controller to affix it onto its stand. "I have to stop—this demo made me that emotional. Whoever made this really captured what it's like to read a script that you love and wanna perform."

Kevin and Malissa take Daniel and Jordan's places in holding Jonah up. Both glance over him with care, as the five exit the break room, ignoring the crowd surging around them.

Daniel waves to passersby. Jordan points to a door leading off the main conference hall. "We made it just in time. Anyone know who it is?" he quickens his pace."

Daniel laughs and shakes his head. "No." He pulls ahead to hold the door open for the others. Jonah trails behind, still shaking. "What's it even about?"

The door glides shut behind them, plunging the group into complete darkness.

Jordan breaks the silence. "How?" No one has time to answer. "How? How'd they do this?"

Jonah strains to pick out his friend as of yesterday, but he fails. He replies in his general direction, "that black paint that blocks almost all—"

"No." Kevin answers. "That costs a fortune. And besides—there's more."

Before anyone can argue, a light begins shining from Kevin's hand—a flashlight, shaking in his clenched fist. "Nice try, handing this to me when I walked in," he jokes to the room beyond.

He spins around, catching each person in the light. As it falls on Daniel, the man lets out a strained laugh. Sweat already glistens on his brow. "Of course. Of course it had to be the Slenderman flashlight. Of course someone gave you that when we came in."

"That's the thing: I didn't feel anyone give it to me. No hands—movement—nothing."

Without warning, Daniel seizes the light from Kevin, who doesn't resist. He aims it around the group but illuminates no one else. He angles it down, searching for a storage box, and as everyone watches, the material underneath them morphs, from linoleum, to tile, even to marble. They edge closer to each other, the surface seeming to rise and fall beneath them, like breathing. Malissa takes Kevin's hand and beckons for everyone to sit in a circle. They're more than happy to oblige.

"Maybe we can bias the results," she explains to him in a firm tone. "This is an immersive experience—not a lecture. The organizer tailored their actions to what you were just doing."

Kevin nods slowly, fingering the flashlight as if it may disappear at any moment. Choosing his words carefully: "So what do they have planned for the rest of us?"

Malissa answers by laying the palm of her free hand on the floor. her colleagues follow. Each winces, as the texture flickers, from smooth marble, to grains of gravel rising between their fingers, even to the coarse grain of hardwood. She dips her free hand into her pocket, emerging with a multitool. Kevin flinches back but doesn't let go of her. Daniel gives her a concerned look. She stares him down, daring him to stop her vandalism, the only way she knows how to assuage her friends' fears.

He relents.

She digs the tip of the blade into the wood, prying a sliver up. When the floor morphs into dirt, blades of grass and all, she repeats the procedure: The knife comes away, speckled with it. She holds both samples, one in each hand.

Emboldened, Jonah knocks his knuckles on the floor between his knees. The dull thud of marble, crunch of gravel, and hollow reverberation of hardwood reach him.

He turns pale. He mouths, Daniel aping in recognition. "Resonance, just like Resonance."

Jonah leans in, his and Kevin's fingers hovering over Malissa's findings, their breath quickening in the otherwise empty room. The composer and voice actor search the other's face for a sign they're hallucinating or overreacting.

They find none.

Jordan fills the silence. "Gen AI can make short films—NPCs—even mimic art and writing styles—but... ."

As Kevin begins to panic, Jordan stands. A headlamp appears on his head as his friends watch. He adjusts the beam's angle, so it shines around the room—

The beam doesn't fall on surrounding walls, filled or empty rows of chairs, or even a podium. Instead, pinpoints of light greet him, blinking in constant rhythm. The longer he stares, the more he sees, until an entire livestreaming setup conjures before his eyes. In silence, he indicates for his friends to watch. Even Kevin obeys. All five pairs of eyes fall on a gaming computer and monitor, its twin occupying a space beside it, floating in midair. It displays the group's faces, without any lag. The stream chat scrolls underneath, containing audience members from the GDC attendees. The computer has every standard part, except a casing.

Jordan begins to signal, but even before he finishes, each person grabs hold of the monitors, wrenches on their sides, and smashes their fists and feet against the screens. Neither of them incurs damage or even moves.

Without prompting, Daniel turns around and rushes toward where the door should be. His fingers scrabble across the wall, its makeup flickering at his touch. He bangs on it with his fists, even headbutting it. Again, and again, and again, he rams first one shoulder, then the other, into the wall, screaming. "My team's trapped! Free them! I'll do anything!"

Only when Jordan drapes his jacket over the camera and streaming setup, do Keven, Malissa, and Jonah drag Daniel away, setting him down between them. None of them flinches, as his frantic blows continue, raining down on all of them with all his strength. Only after obscuring the camera does Jordan join Kevin and Jonah on the floor, eyes brimming with tears along with them. Daniel can't tear his gaze away from his friends: Their collective distress at once brings him to a stop and racks him with sobs.

Malissa retrieves Daniel's phone. She holds it up to his face just long enough to unlock it and posts an identical message to all of his social media accounts, pausing between each word. Daniel doesn't stop her whatsoever, even as she snaps unedited photos of his bruise body and tearful face. She does the same for the others' phones, socials, and photos. She concludes each post with a QR code to the still active stream.

'Thank you for making the last three days the best of my life. Of my friends' lives. I want to spend the rest of my life with you. But not in joy, not in fear. There is never enough time to do the things you want to do, once you've found them. But you all helped me find them. Thank you. And goodbye.'

Malissa doesn't have to speak, or even move, after posting all the messages. Jordan seizes her arm, eyes fixed on the streaming setup. The group doesn't intervene, as Jordan's jacket lifts off the screen and camera. Boxy, yet dexterous, metal claws flick at the jacket.

Jordan stands in front of Daniel's still prone body, arms spread. Kevin joins him, wielding the flashlight like a club. Malissa unveils the longest knife from her multitool. Jonah removes his name tag lanyard and earphones, weaves the strands together, and forms them into a garotte.

Jordan glares at the camera, quaking with rage. "Tell us what you want with him! You *fuck!*"

The featureless darkness around them solidifies. A figure appears.

Even in perfect lighting, its appearance melds from one form to another. Its height, build, hair, skin, and eye color, and even skeletal structure changing as the group watches. However, with each one, at least one member of the group's mouth falls open in shock. Multiple times, someone whispers a phrase to the effect of, "How did you get that beta design? I never talked or wrote about it. I dreamed it."

The figure doesn't respond, not to the group. Instead, its voice resonates in a chorus of tones, but each person only hears one.

It turns to Kevin, arms spread in welcome. "Help me resonate with your fans, deliver a relatable, novel performance."

Malissa transfixes on the figure, who gestures with a pen with one limb, and completes dexterous, rapid inputs via a controller with the other. Even the controller's shape melds between forms as she watches. "We'll create an experience that pushes players' skills to their limits. We'll reward their knowledge. But simultaneously we'll uplift whoever's struggling."

Daniel's mouth falls open. He sees no one. Instead, a quiet, yet intense tone addresses him, the voice seeming to come from a pair of bright eyes in the darkness. Even without a visible body, he knows it's leaning in toward him. "Our narrative will transport players. Just as you have done. But we won't suffer those unwilling to expend the effort to humor us. We will seek out worthy challengers for you—our game deserves nothing less."

KÁRMÁN'S GARROTE

The first volunteer throws up—or almost does, seconds away from damaging equipment worth millions of dollars. Helpless, the Secret Service watches as the president pales and gives the signal to stop the centrifuge. Its current velocity and acceleration don't simulate weightlessness on earth.

Among themselves, the Secret service at once jokes and worries about the president's failure to meet the expectations they set for the public.

Even after the president embraces that failure, and gives a press conference. Shaking, sweating, but optimistic, the other civilian passengers don't respect the mission. Identical scenes play out dozens of times worldwide, at training setups that fulfill the same tasks. Few endure the true G-forces on the first pass, the second, or the third. The intensity soon sobers the leaders with pilot's licenses, of civilian and military aircraft, as well. Everyone struggles to keep conscious, let alone calm, as the stresses on their bodies peak.

Nonetheless, the participants crawl forward, toward the mandatory thresholds.

The prerequisite technological developments manifest faster than anyone expected. CERN, the ESA, and NASA exchange data and aggregate funds. Applications for nuclear physicists, aerospace engineers, and related professions, overrun job boards. Nuclear technicians gain recognition, if not celebrity status, as their families and friends inquire into nuclear fusion's role in rocket propulsion.

Workers in STEM fields don't hoard the spotlight, however. Communication experts, linguists, psychologists, and even members of entertainment industries, carve out niches. They debate which works of science, art, and news the eligible group of world leaders should consume while in space. They even argue over where those works should go on the station caring for the James Webb Space Telescope, sitting at the second Lagrange Point of the sun and earth.

The team broadcasts its intent to coincide the launch with a refueling mission, which stabilizes the station's orbit about every three weeks. Newsroom chatter's telegraph cadence, universal across languages, rides the airwaves and floods every social media and content creation website. Cameras of all shapes and sizes, and crowds of physical and remote camera operators, jockey for the best spots in a loose perimeter around the launch platform in international waters. Flotillas, comprised of allied militaries, protect all gathered scientific and media personnel.

Explanations of the tug of war between chemical and physical forces engulf viewers and listeners' cars, homes, and classrooms. The employees at for-profit companies who offered their expertise silence their public relations departments' incessant self-promotion. However many times the mission control and media staff have seen crewed launches, awe and anxiety loom large. They sublimate when the capsule attains earth's escape velocity—seven miles per second.

It wins the tug of war.

Earth's atmospheric density breaks equilibrium, the portion above it less dense than below it. The captain and crew confirm mission control's overjoyed radio transmissions. Yes— the capsule has reached space and can continue its journey.

No amount of training diminishes the spectacle for the passengers. The vibrations shuddering through the capsule, the acceleration pressing them against their seat backs, the drop of their collective stomachs, culminate in extraplanetary weightlessness. In geostationary orbit, They overlook the pale blue dot.

Only now, does anyone vocalize, let alone speak. Three politicians, separated by thousands of miles and even decades of experience, embrace. They're undeterred by the awkwardness of microgravity, or the fabric and fiber optics of their spacesuits crinkling against each other.

Everyone's speeches, written while censored by gravity, proceed without issue, including cathartic cry breaks over the view. A flock of translators conveys them to their grounded audience. Some actors and authors even respond using constructed languages designed around spacefaring civilizations. Corrections over pronunciation and disposition happen, of course, but all in good humor.

The man's heavy, unbroken strides through the crowd don't raise suspicion, not until he approaches the airlock. The NASA and Roscosmos crew chide him, beckoning him back to the group, but he remains stone-faced. His eyes flick to the view through the windows, of earth shrinking in on itself against the vacuum of space. No one halts him or thinks of deactivating his security clearance.

His training to open the inner airlock doors succeeds.

No one moves as he seals the airlock behind him and strips off his spacesuit and the helmet flattening his short, brown hair. His dark suit, matching white dress shirt and silk tie, and dress shoes, follow. He stows everything in a locker. His state physician, helpless to stop him, gawks as his space suit's readings fall away. Only the fiber optic sensors in his trousers transmit data anymore.

No one notices the second man, marching the same path as the first.

The passengers realize where he's going. Screams ring out.

Hands lunge toward him, straining to pull him back, but the shock from the first man's actions weighs them down. He outpaces the invading parties, unsealing the inner airlock doors with one hand and discarding his blue tie with the other.

An Israeli flag pin affixed to it clinks against the floor outside the airlock.

The second man's eyes rivet on the closest window. He strips down and stores his space suit, navy business suit, and shoes, in a locker next to the first man's belongings. When finished, he's adorned in a white dress shirt and black pants.

The men don't look at each other.

Each enacts their trainers' instructions, securing their tethers, earmarked for use at the station, around their waists. Some slack in each line wraps around their clenched fists.

With a blank expression, his square jaw set, the first man opens the chamber's outer door, the newcomer close behind. The leaders' entourages don't stop them from embracing the smothering vacuum of space. The grounded media personnel gape but can't help but film them.

Both turn their backs to the cameras, the first man's upper body laid bare, the second still covered.

Each exhales as long as they can.

Only cringes of agony, from the capsule and video conferencing news media, break up the ensuing two minutes of silence. The skin of the men's arms and backs bloat. The gases dissolved in their blood, nowhere near boiling point in terrestrial conditions, expand. The reduced boiling point in the vacuum drives those gases outward.

Sensors from both men's trousers alert their transfixed physicians to blood vessel ruptures and tissue ebullism. After ten seconds, both men go slack, unconscious.

The water in their blood boils next, its stored heat energy escaping their concealed nostrils and mouths into the void. Even their highest ranking officials avert their eyes from the wisps of vapor rising around their bare heads. The sensors record plummeting body temperatures and oxygen content. Lung deflation. Asphyxiation.

Their brains die. Their hearts stop.

The garrote loosens.

INTERSECTIONS

I open my eyes, but not from sleep.

My joints crack as I sit up toward the smog-laced sky, and the people bustling around me. A diverse cross section of individuals of different ages, cultures, and degrees of urgency, rush by. The pavement rumbles, imperceptible—or perhaps, unimportant—to the pedestrians. It takes a minute before I register the insistent buzzing across my chest, and the alert nudging the inside of my skull.

A subway train passed by underneath me. I'm early.

I stow the tablet strapped across my full-body harness and search for a sign or billboard. I grin from ear to ear. The unassuming street sign welcomes me to Manhattan, even as commuters ignore the transparent film over my clothes, mask on my face, and bioelectronic implants protruding from my limbs and skull.

I start to walk, pulling sunglasses from my pocket and

pulling them down over my eyes. In the same motion, I tweak a dial embedded in one of my cheekbones. The graphs snake across the inside of the sunglasses' lenses and my own eyelids— the worldlines of every person I passed by and look at in real time. Their locations in space and time manifest as lines on a graph. Even as I watch, the computer at my hip and in my skull scrubs their names and faces from its databases; I can't bring personally identifiable information of private citizens back with me , after all. I take manual notes on my tablet, unassisted by generative AI, wandering through the city along the most prominent sets of worldlines.

The glinting, metal barricades in the sun catch my attention. I stop and gape for a moment but change course as the police usher pedestrians along ahead of me. Instead, I stop at a park across the street from the state courthouse. Protesters flock nearby, holding up signs saying "lock him up". On the other side of the chain link fence, a smaller group of supporters display signs reading "four more years" and "witch hunt". I glance at the worldline display and eavesdrop on reporters across the street, thumbing a touchpad behind each ear.

"Historic—"

"First trial of a former president—"

"Two-thousand sixteen election interference case—"

"Jury selection—"

I sway in place, my knees growing wobbly underneath me, even as the augmented joints labor to right me. In a secure browser, I connect to the internet—this time period's internet—and perform a short set of searches: The current date, president, and the most high profile trials at this time. As the text scrolls across my brain-computer interface, the time and place click all at once. The time and place aren't abstract, pinpoints on a hand drawn timeline on the wall of my office. As I tap into the news reporters' streams of visuals, and allow it to immerse me, the gravity of the situation grows clear.

I reach out and graze Judge Juan Merchan's face, before withdrawing it, embarrassed at the violation of personal space. I smile at him instead, intent on his every word. Legal stationary on my lap, I take notes as thorough as if I was a juror. Never mind that one hasn't been paneled yet.

I silence my devices. Judge Merchan's smooth, calm voice at once washes over me and jolts me to attention. Not even the glitches in virtual reality around me, visual and auditory, dampen my enthusiasm or draw me away from the trial creeping closer, blocks away.

At the end of the first day of jury selection, the motel owner doesn't bat an eye as I slide a wad of cash across the counter. She doesn't even look my way, as I leave my room at five in the morning every day for the next six or seven weeks. I return to the same park every day of trial—hell, even on off days—to absorb the atmosphere. My worldline data grows more refined. I can correlate clusters of lines to different groups of people: Reporters, law enforcement, and the court staff themselves. My outline lengthens and fills out each day, packed with details only an attendee in the courthouse would know. Iover those weeks, my point of view character shifts. It starts as a reporter, vigilant and on edge, torturing their keyboard as they relay the news to their co-anchors in studio. As much as I respect the press, and even the one reporter I fixate on, I can't place myself in his shoes. He's too distant from the proceedings, however objective and reassuring his accounts sound.

As the prosecution rests its case, I transition to individuals inside the courthouse. From interviews I watch while lying in bed at the end of the day, the group of sketch artists catches my attention. Their words serve as art as well as their visual representations. No matter how long I listen to them describe the frustrating yet rewarding process of depicting the court proceedings, I can't see myself writing like them. I'm no artist, with pastels or BCI projections.

Only on the last day, when the news breaks, do I settle on my point of view. Separated by aging, austere concrete walls and security perimeters, his voice rings out, soft and clear, but authoritative. He announces that the jury has a verdict, and that they want to fill out the jury forms. Judge Merchan sits back at the bench, and from my place on my own park bench, my smile shrinks into a line of concentration. I free write what he sounds like, looks like, how he carries himself.

The half hour whizzes by. Once the foreman of the jury begins reading out the verdict, one count at a time, I let myself bask in the moment, like everyone else. I soak in the cheers and jeers from the protesters, of all kinds. Even so, eyes never leave Judge Merchan's worldline. Just like the seven prior weeks, he remains calm and composed, but from my vantage point, the slightest hints of shock and relief, and the weight of solemnity, reach me.

In few words, he thanks the jury. I tear up as his voice pierces my virtual reality space, recreating the courtroom. I mouth, "thank you", as I leave the bench and walk away.

My hands work at the electronics attached to my body. I'm ready to return home. *My audience deserves to witness this slice of history without bias or desecration.*

The hardware and software on and around me jolt to life, and I close my eyes. A message to my publicist and editor races ahead and behind me. 'I narrowed the scope of my manuscript, like you asked. Just one more thing to do. Then I'll meet you at home.'

I open my eyes, relieved that I've returned to the right place. I set the last page of my notes on Judge Merchan's grave, over graffiti someone reapplied in my absence.

LEAPS INTO FAITH

I wave goodbye to the employees the register, maintaining the façade of a smile as they haul away my donations. Clothing, furniture, and even my old TV, cross the event horizon of the Goodwill doors.

The warm, fuzzy optimism over bettering my neighbor's lives with my junk, and cleaning out my house all at once, dissipates. My façade crumbles.

My confident posture slumps, as I start my engine and crank up my music. Sunshades duct taped to the windows of my car hide my tortured expression from prying eyes. I tread my anxiety like water. A female voice muses to herself, her voice almost whispering in my ear from the back seat. I mouth along, driving home to my reconciliation, or execution. *"Two choices on my mind, four hours on the road. Give way to control."*

TAKE WHAT I WANT, THEN LEAVE

My hand hovers over my key fob. With effort, I yank it free and trek to my front door. The dirge echoes between my ears, even as the ice, liquor, and hot chocolate, fall into place: Calm amidst the surrounding turbulence. Procrastination coaxes me to my bedroom, silencing the last vestiges of caution, like my phone, cradled in its charging dock. "One game," I reassure no one. "Then I'll tell them everything."

Mitosis divides one game into two. Two games divide into four. Four games divide into sixteen.

My runaway mitosis sweeps me up for one hour, two, four. In the fifth hour, exhausted from a losing streak spanning my favorite games, I make my second drink. This time, I mix Kahlua, and Bailey's in a glass, filling the rest with whipped cream. "I give you... a blowjob." I present the drink with a flourish to no one, plopping it onto a bar that doesn't exist.

Drink in hand, I exhume my college laptop from storage. Sluggish, rotten, academic and recreational writing rises from the grave, every word jeering as I read it. Back then, my biases magnified my problems. They felt as numerous as they were important. I created with maximum effort, at the peak of my current skills, preserving my successes and failures in amber.

My archived art and music conjure more intense emotions. Cringing, I force myself to scrutinize my song lyrics to hip hop and electronic albums that looped in my head: Not in front of crowds of thousands of people. Fan art and albums—

legal and pirated—from game and film soundtracks, revive my love of franchises that I forgot that I loved in the first place. A fond smile creeps across my face, as I confirm the download dates and genre tags on each song.

Splayed across the floor, on my new laptop, I pull up my YouTube watch history, prioritizing material from the past ten years. My favorite creators, past and present, flit past. I grin from ear to ear at some faces. Others I give the middle finger to before clicking off them, or allow a resigned sigh to slip between my teeth. I punch the screen and one man's channel banner with my fist and cursor. In spite of my roiling emotions, the catharsis guides my remaining work.

Now, my artistic and fandom life sprawls across dozens of tabs. Among my writing, art and music, and videos, I isolate the entries I'm least proud of, that I'm angry that I enjoyed, that I'm disappointed in. I drag them into a folder labeled 'My Worst'. In each item's metadata or annotations, I justify, or excuse, my hesitancy in sharing this item sooner in our relationship.

I juxtapose them with a second folder, 'My Best'. It shelters fifty percent more items, and its explanations total twice as many words as 'My Worst'.

I transport everything onto a portable hard drive and archive the load in a .zip folder, named 'Snapshot'.

In my excitement, I kick my chair over and across the room. I haul my table lamp back where it belongs. I revert my room back to normal. *You have to see me for who I am.*

I take a selfie: My wrinkled clothes, my unkempt hair, my face flushed from a second Blowjob, created and consumed before I reintroduced myself to my old short stories. I transmit the unedited image to my new computer and package it in the .zip folder. I attach it to a blank Entropy message. Tears of drunken, anxious relief spill down my face, as I gulp a glass of ice water and purge my emotions in a cold shower.

I don't check the time when I fall asleep or wake up. Light floods through my window, my eyes creaking open. At the top of my laptop screen, a notification greets me.

My friend replied an hour ago: 'Here's mine.'

They attach a .zip folder. The folder and file names are identical to mine, except for one video.

I laugh in shock, shedding my residual emotions. The burden of disclosing myself lifts from my shoulders. I open and pause the attached video at the start, a favor for my future self, as I fall back asleep, sober and at peace.

This time, it takes two hours to wake up again, a second to play the video, my laptop balancing on my chest, and a minute to lug my suitcase out of my closet. My friend trembles, phone aimed at their face. They spin once around their room, opening every poster, every figurine, every family and friend group photo to scrutiny. They stop, gazing out their window. To the camera, they ask, holding back tears: "Did you take the week off—no. It doesn't matter.

"Because I did. I'll top off my gas tank on the way over. I don't care what you're doing. I'll be there."

They kneel and pack a bag, the top one in a pile of suitcases and backpacks. A stuffed garbage bag peeks out from the rest of their belongings. As they roll up a shirt and nestle it inside, they turn to the camera again. "I don't care where you wanna go—hell I'll stay at your house while you're at work, if you want. Just tell me where."

I smile. I pause, a bundle of shirts clenched in one fist. I nod toward the video before replying, my fingers shaking.

"I will."

They send me location tracking data—they left ten minutes ago. Attached is a Spotify code and a video of them racing down the highway, windows down.

They wanted to see me. My flaws didn't matter to them. I can't hear their joy over the wind, but I can read the declaration in the caption.

"Because sometimes in love—you've got to take the leap. Just hold on to me."

AN INTERVIEW WITH PAULINE UGALDE

1. When did you start writing and why?

I began writing short stories as homework in second or third grade. I experimented with fanfiction writing in third or fourth grade, by writing blogs and comments from readers, fake usernames and all. I anticipated freewriting time and chafed at writing fiction while under time pressure and following a prompt.

I didn't develop a daily writing habit until seventh grade. Except for my senior year of high school and first year of college, I've written creatively a majority of days each week.

2. Which authors or books or media influenced you the most as a writer?

The Harry Potter franchise's fanfiction.net subdivision influenced me as a writer because I learned how to apply content filters and curate my preferences. One metanarrative story about an author's characters revolting against their author, due to his negligence writing his stories and characters' personalities, stuck with me until now. The author identified, parodied, and critiqued fanfiction conventions, and each character expressed dissatisfaction with them. Instead of preaching to the audience, the author created emotional connections. I valued the characters' concerns and took them to heart.

As my tastes evolved, I valued authors who could convey dense worldbuilding in an entertaining way. The examples that affected me were the low fantasy *Inheritance Cycle* by Christopher Paolini, and the science fiction series *Time's Eye* by Arthur C. Clark. Both framed worldbuilding as character building moments. As I grew up, I appreciated Paolini creating a world map and multiple constructed languages. Since I read *Time's Eye*, I respected the science I learned from Clark, and how he linked his research to his story.

In high school, I paired my entrance into the horror genre with finding a website called Television Tropes and Idioms. It exposed me to media and genre conventions. Its trope description articles are equally informative and funny, and feature user submitted examples from diverse media. I saw how different creators utilized each trope.

This format proved its worth after I read *Carrie*, by Steven King, my first found footage story, and read about the first *Saw* film, released in 2004, my first horror franchise. Both contained never-before-seen tropes and storytelling genre conventions. I even found books by film and literary scholars analyzing both works, like how I analyzed books in school. These scholars validated my enjoyment and emboldened me to write about my favorite fandoms.

My horror fandom deepened in college when I watched Jordan Peele's 2017 film *Get Out* with my cousins, the first horror film I watched blind. *Get Out* taught me how to blend Humor and suspense with horror. Though I learned similar techniques from the first *Scream* film, which I watched earlier that year, I knew the plot already, so I watched it to see the it in context.

During Christmas break 2017, I watched the then-current eight *Saw* films for the first time. I enjoyed the fandom because of the behind the scenes effort. Tobin Bell's interviews about playing John Kramer were educational but not pretentious. He taught me about method acting and how to write morally questionable, compelling characters.

After college, I found multiple works I took inspiration from and creators who I admired. I listened to a fan-created audiobook of *House of Leaves*, by Mark Z. Danielewski. I loved how he blended print media and film formatting conventions, to enforce his book's themes. I also found the YouTube channel *Dead Meat*, which releases the *Kill Count* web series. The hosts explain horror films' plot, production, and history in the context of the deaths depicted in them.

Simultaneously, I found the fiction I didn't like, and saw

examples of the traits I didn't want in my work. A friend sent me an accessible version of Andrew Hussie's webcomic and web series hybrid *Homestuck*, adapted by fans. Fans described each comic panel, and paired them with *Homestuck*'s text. Reading Homestuck like a novel was as frustrating as it was informative. Without the visuals, the tonally confusing, detailed, and shoddy writing, took precedent. I quit reading partway through, angry at Hussie for wasting my time and squandering the aspects that I enjoy. I felt cheated for investing in a work that seemed both more serious and satirical than in reality. He elaborated on his world via thousands of words of intriguing, yet extraneous and unrefined details. He included scenes that confused me without any plot or artistic justification. *Homestuck* was the first work I read where the author didn't edit it enough, and or didn't ask an editor to do so. I resolved to make accessible, experimental fiction, with accommodations that didn't compromise the work.

The creators who impacted me most creatively were Toby Fox, the writer and developer for the indie RPGs *Undertale* and *Deltarune*, and Daniel Mullins, specifically his 2021 psychological horror, deckbuilding, escape room game *Inscryption*. *Undertale* was my first metanarrative video game. The humor resonated with me since Fox translated jokes like those in *Scream* to RPGs.

Mullins distilled the pacing and content aspects I enjoyed, with the most frustrating creative choices from *Homestuck*, into one game. As a horror fan, I didn't think any work of fiction could scare me or affect me as emotionally as Inscryption. When I played it with an online friend, the dialogue scared me within the first few seconds. The game's tone and content reminded me of *Get Out*. The payoff was satisfying, in spite of some game design and storytelling choices harming my experience in an attempt to create an immersive world.

3. Which authors or books or media had the biggest impact on you as a person?

Though *Harry Potter* was the first fandom I consumed content for and made friends over, I didn't participate in in fandom until high school. TV Tropes taught me about fandom, so I could engage with it in a deliberate way.

In college, most of the same fiction that influenced me as a writer influenced me as a person. *Undertale* and *Deltarune* led to me making new friends in shared fandoms, and grappling with the relationship between a creator and their fans. I gained and lost friends over these two games since I failed to manage my emotions about them. Even now, I'm ashamed of my behavior and strive to manage those feelings, so I don't drive away more people I care about.

Conversely, watching the *Saw* franchise during that period's presidential administration solidified my values. I resented people who took their sight for granted. I grew frustrated with people who asked well-meaning, stupid questions about blind people. I learned the truth in John

Kramer's philosophy and methods, that "those who do not appreciate life do not deserve life", without minimizing his flaws. I excerpted the songs *Gold*, by Excision & Illenium, Featuring Shallows, and *Don't Look Down*, by Excision, Wooli, & Codeko.

During the COVID-19 pandemic, a *Game of Thrones* quote strengthened these realizations. *"There is only one god. And his name is death. And there is only one thing we say to death: Not today."* During and after the pandemic, I witnessed people who didn't appreciate other people's lives. My friends and I were disheartened by the futility of our efforts to minimize COVID's spread, and the virus' mutations removing our ability to socialize without fear. *"Not today"* filled a gap in Kramer's philosophy: I couldn't guarantee that others would appreciate my life. Therefore, I had to live each day as if it were my last.

Inscryption influenced me as a person and as a creator. I played the game at the then current, lowest point of my life. I never properly grieved an extended family member's death of COVID-19 in 2020. I didn't know her well. Her death shattered the surrealness of the pandemic. Technical difficulties at the funeral prevented me from listening to it. My repress feelings flooded out at the end of *Inscryption*, when I met each of the remaining main characters, while the game deleted itself. I grieved one character's death, after He confirms that *"once [he] is deleted, it is truly over for [him]. But [I] will live to see more."*

This dialogue and situation mirrored the news stories

about loved ones video calling loved ones to say goodbye, to avoid contracting COVID. I began crying. My attention on the game broke. The full force and catharsis of my grief overcame me.

4. Which of your original twelve *Prompt* stories are you most pleased with?

I'm proud of my October 2023 story, since I threaded the needle regarding how to pay homage to the *Saw* franchise without making blatant references that disrupted the plot. Learning screenwriting and writing multiple short stories helped me identify the most iconic moments from the script and play with readers' expectations.

I'm proud of *Kármán's Garrote* since it was my best political wish fulfillment story and inspired by a 2022 Neil DeGrasse Tyson interview on *The Late Show with Stephen Colbert*, where he describes the overview effect. He wishes he could drag every world leader up into low earth orbit to experience it. *Kármán's Garrote* required research into terrestrial astronaut training and space flight during the first half, and spacesuits and the vacuum of space's physiological effects during the second half. Even after rigorous editing, the story felt disjointed until I lengthened my planned ending to include another political leader committing suicide via vacuum.

Leaps into Faith describes how I'd want to introduce

myself to an online friend if I had ample time and emotional strength. I'd want that friend to know about the worst and best parts of me before committing. I played with portrayals of friendships and romantic relationships, by excerpting lyrics that discuss romantic relationships at different stages. After my boyfriend and I got together, I wasn't interested in writing romantic relationships. It dawned on me how cheesy, superficial, and or overdramatic most portrayals of romances are. I began writing about close friendships instead, especially friend groups. Even after forming one in high school, I felt lonely by default.

Overall, *Delusion* is the story I'm most proud of since it's the first time I synthesized my learning from both my creative writing and generative AI classes. This manifested in not only the character of QUINN, a generative AI utilizing quantum computing, but also that I used GPT 3.5 for character names. Asking a generative AI for suggestions forced me to write a clear, concise summary my story. This process solidified how valuable generative AI would be in my professional and artistic pursuits, and how vital it was that I learned to do so properly.

5. Which of your original twelve *Prompt* stories did you find the most difficult to write?

November and December 2023's stories were the most difficult to write because of being fired from one of my freelance writing jobs, and the onset the Israel-Hamas war.

I had *at least* one nightmare about the news coverage. I inevitably wrote horror with a hopeless tone. *Don't Wake Up*, my November story, and *It's You and Me that Matter*, my December story, were my bleakest stories, sharing both subject matter and tone. The primary difference is that *It's You and Me that Matter* has fewer characters.

Though almost all my *Prompt* submissions contain at least one character death, they're either more surreal or have a happier ending. More than any other time during *Prompt*, my stories reflected my prevailing emotions, but I also struggled to express them.

On one hand, I'm proud that I processed my trauma by creating art. On the other hand, I'm demoralized that the stories that diverged farthest from my comfort zone stemmed from trauma. No matter how responsible I felt to stay abreast of current events by watching daily news, I couldn't express my sinking horror and dread except through fiction.

6. What book on writing do you recommend?

I learned in high school that I didn't know enough about writing to curate the advice I read in writing books. What I found came off as haughty, a professional writer forgetting how to address a newcomer. Instead, I learned by reading and watching metanarratives, in print and film, and reading their TV Tropes pages. Each work is as instructive as it is entertaining, and its trope page elaborates on it, without sounding didactic.

If you can take online writing courses, I recommend University of Michigan's Good with Words: Writing and Editing specialization, and Wesleyan University's Creative Writing Specialization, distributed through Coursera. They teach writing logistics practices applicable to all forms of writing, creative writing included.

7. What advice would you give an unpublished writer?

My advice involves the writing logistics. As much as possible, write every day—even if it's only for a couple of minutes or a page. Skipping a day occasionally is okay, as long as designated daily writing period are as long and productive as is reasonable.

To establish this habit, find the time, place, and setup where you can write consistently and uninterrupted. Once you find it, you'll increase the mental energy allocated toward writing, not *preparing* to write.

Regardless of a project's length, allocate ample time to research, complete the first draft, edit, and so on, and set deadlines between each step. Without deadlines, you'll procrastinate. Without ample time, you'll rush to complete each one. End each writing session by writing the first sentence of the next paragraph or section. Leaving unfinished work will motivate you to continue it next time.

Identify the most distinct, your favorite, and least favorite aspects of your most loved works of fiction or nonfiction. You can either emulate or avoid them. Reading, watching, or playing metanarratives from your favorite media or genres can also highlight common and novel tropes in your favorite media or genres. Metannaratives can shape the types of stories you want to write.

8. Do you have a "dream project" as a writer? What would it be?

Though I would love to write a horror game, my dream project is writing a horror film. I'd collaborate with James A. Janisse, the primary host of the *Kill Count on the Dead Meat* YouTube channel, and one host of the podcast of the same name; Kevin Williamson, the writer for the first *Scream* film and the 2024 horror comedy *Totally Killer*; or the directors Jordan Peele, James Wan, or Leigh Whannell. The hypothetical metanarrative horror film would have ample gore, visceral sound design, and a smart script that actors improved by developing character backstory.

Charlie Clouser, the *Saw* franchise's composer, Jonah Senzel, the sole composer for game developer Daniel Mullins as of 2023, *Disasterpeace*, the musician for the 2014 film *IT Follows*, and/or Spencer Charnas, the frontman of the metalcore band *Ice Nine Kills*, would compose the score.

Regardless of horror subgenre, the film's viral marketing campaign would be accessible. I could appreciate if I was a viewer. I'd create written and audio descriptions of marketing materials and events. These documents, videos, and press appearances, like those for *The Blair Witch Project*, would provide worldbuilding for the plot. Physical releases for the film must be meaningful—not art books or alternate packaging alone. The cast and crew would host both scheduled and spontaneous events nationwide, at diverse venues, including virtual appearances with horror content creators.

9. Your stories will be published in a set of *Prompt* collections with the other Third Generation authors but also as a collection of just your own work. Did you have a conscious theme for your personal collection?

During *Prompt*, I was working and job searching, so I listed a few potential ideas the day I received each phrase and the next day, drafted an outline based on one. The final topic derived from the most compelling actions I took, thoughts I had, and YouTube or news I consumed, in the preceding week. Rarely, the topic came from what happened in the proceeding couple days. I didn't want to waste time brainstorming or drafting, so I stuck to the horror genre, crossed with science fiction or low fantasy. I also knew I could write stories containing violence and or death well, so I capitalized on those strengths.

Regardless of genre, I also restricted my submissions to small casts, with *Instantly Rehabilitated* and *Delusion* being intentional exceptions. I incremented the cast size in the former story, since I wanted each video call to represent a distinct emotion Dr. Mehmet Dagen's patients felt. From the beginning, I framed *Delusion* as a modern day Stephen King short story, in the same vein as the Duffer brothers, the Netflix *show Stranger Things'* creators, did for their stylized depiction of the 1980s. I both added as many named characters as I could within reason, and named them after characters from King's works.

I also only wrote two stories, *Amphoteric* and *Don't Wake Up*, with extended crowd scenes, and only the latter featured a crowd described in detail. After the COVID-19 pandemic and the January sixth insurrection, I associated crowds with mistrusting strangers and angry people, so I avoided writing them. These two stories were the exceptions since I wrote *Amphoteric* in reverse: I imagined a mass death scene at the end of Amphoteric, so I depicted it.

In *Don't Wake Up*, I wanted to portray a crowd's reactions to the emergency alert system activating and communication systems overloading, so a crowd was mandatory. The opening scene of Michael Grant's young adult novel *Gone*, where panicking students gather in the hallways and futilely call their parents, inspired *Don't Wake Up's* opening.

10. Who do you write for and how does it drive you to create?

I write because I want to create fiction I myself would read or watch, if I found them in the wild. Early in my horror fandom, I realized that I enjoyed works that lack mass appeal. I shocked people when I told them about my favorite horror movies. At the same time, I watched *Janisse* and *Dead Meat* pair niche content with effective viewer retention strategies, cultivating a loyal following. I also respected Wan and Whannell's writing and pitching process for the first *Saw* film. These creators inform how I balance artistic integrity and pragmatism.

11. Optimally, we're always growing and improving as authors. Talk about how you grew or changed as a writer over the course of creating your stories for *Prompt: The Third Generation*.

In the first quarter of 2024, I enrolled in two online course specializations: About writing and editing, and creative writing specifically. About halfway through *Prompt's* duration, the fast turnaround wore me down and stunted my ability to draft and edit consistently. A law professor taught the Writing and Editing specialization by detailing productivity improvements employed by authors and filmmakers. This methodology cemented the specialization's value.

I'd written fiction consistently for more than fifteen years but only began receiving compensation in 2021. I took a specialization that provided guidance on creative writing logistics to output higher quality work faster. I know I wouldn't have persevered through Prompt's challenges if I hadn't completed both specializations simultaneously.

12.   Imagine the perfect cover for your personal collection. Describe it... even if it's impossible.

The black, textured cover responds to haptic and infrared stimulus. A reader must touch the design to decipher it. Marketing materials would elaborate on the factors that change the design, not the design itself. Those factors may even change across printings or versions of the book, turning them into collector's items with genuine differences between them.